"We'll have to go into quarantine."

Cliff Sinclair, the brilliant surgeon, tersely announced the outbreak of bubonic plague in the Mallison hospital in Egypt.

It was all Shannon could do to control her reaction to the dread disease. But as administrator of the hospital she had to be an example to everyone else. She had to remain cool at all costs.

The quarantine meant days of working side by side with Cliff, facing death every moment. She was engaged to another man, so she had to conceal her growing love for Cliff—but how could she, when every day was so precious?

Other

MYSTIQUE BOOKS

by LILIANE ROBIN

For a free catalogue listing all available Mystique Books,
send your name and address to:

MYSTIQUE BOOKS,
M.P.O. Box 707, Niagara Falls, N.Y. 14302
In Canada: 649 Ontario St., Stratford, Ontario N5A 6W2

Night of the Scorpion

by LILIANE ROBIN

MYSTIQUE BOOKS

TORONTO · LONDON · NEW YORK
HAMBURG · AMSTERDAM · STOCKHOLM

NIGHT OF THE SCORPION/first published August 1980

ISBN 0-373-50092-0

PRINTED IN U.S.A.

Chapter 1

"Dr. Mallison, Dr. Shannon Mallison," the voice droned over the intercom. "Report to Dr. Charles Mallison's office immediately."

Dr. Shannon Mallison raised her head, a tense, worried look clouding her gray eyes. Why did they keep paging her; she wondered. Why didn't the nurse come to relieve her?

The young Egyptian woman on the bed before her groaned and writhed violently in a futile effort to escape the pain.

"Look at me," Shannon said urgently, stroking the child-filled belly and claiming the woman's attention with her eyes. The patient's sweat-streaked face turned upward, her wild eyes riveted on the doctor's, her wracked body easing slowly into a controlled peace.

"Dr. Mallison, Dr. Shannon Mallison," the high-pitched voice repeated for the fourth time. "Please report to Dr. Charles Mallison's office immediately. Urgent." the voice added, betraying an edge of panic.

What could be wrong? Her grandfather had never called her to his office in this way before. Impatiently, she pressed the call button once again. Why was it taking so long for help to come? There was no way she could leave her patient. This was not an easy labor; the baby's position was dangerous and all the mother's strength and cooperation would soon be needed to assure a safe birth. If the woman gave in to her pain, all would be lost.

The contraction passed. The woman closed her eyes, her need for rest after twelve hours of hard labor so overwhelming that, between her bouts with pain, she became oblivious to all around her, lapsing into a brief sleep.

Shannon knew it would only be a minute before they had to tackle the next hurdle.

"Rest now," she murmured in a calming tone, maintaining her hand's relaxing circular motion on the taut belly. For a second she thought she could feel movement beneath the surface. Was it a boy or a girl, she wondered. Would it be healthy and well? Was this new soul destined to poverty, to a life of starvation, illiteracy and disease? Or would luck and family love provide this tiny being with the gift of a full and happy life? She didn't know. She only knew that the life force was powerful and awesome; it was at moments such as these that she felt humbled by it.

"You are doing very well," she said quietly, knowing the woman was listening. "When the next contraction comes, remember—try to relax, breathe deeply and follow me like you . . . ."

Her instructions were cut off abruptly by the sudden onset of a powerful contraction.

"*Wen-Nabi*—by the prophet!" the young woman called out in the privacy of her pain.

"Breathe," Shannon whispered, holding the woman's gaze, oblivious to the abrupt sound of a door slamming behind her.

"I told you why." The young woman's slurred voice spoke angrily behind Shannon. "Besides, I don't have to answer to you."

"Shh," another voice cautioned. "Quiet . . . ."

"Why? What's the big deal?"

Dr. Shannon Mallison did not move; her eyes could not leave her patient's face. She knew that if she looked away for even a second, her patient's concentration would be broken and the woman would be plunged into blinding pain.

"Shannon," the loud young woman said, grabbing the doctor's arm for attention. "What are you doing here? Granddaddy has summoned you." Her voice lingered sarcastically on "granddaddy," making her contempt obvious.

Shannon watched steadily as her patient passed through the last of the contraction. Then with a weary sigh, she turned to face her visitors.

Ella, a plump, middle-aged woman in a crisp nurse's uniform, stood before her with a stern and disapproving frown on her face.

"I'm sorry I couldn't get here sooner, Dr. Mallison," the nurse rushed to apologize. "But Carol has been causing some difficulty in the dispensary and I had no choice but to get her out of there."

"Don't blame me," the girl said, sulking. She slumped against the wall, her curly red hair covering her impudent green eyes, her lips puckering richly into a pout, her hands falling lazily to her hips. Her slow speech and slight stagger warned Shannon that Carol had probably consumed quite a large quantity of alcohol or drugs. It wasn't the first time it had happened and it was certainly not going to be the last—that the doctor knew.

"It's not even ten o'clock in the morning! Why are you . . . ."

But her words were interrupted by the increasingly anxious voice over the intercom: "Urgent, Dr. Shannon Mallison. Please report to Dr. Charles Mallison's office. Any parties knowing of Dr. Shannon Mallison's whereabouts please report to the front desk. Urgent . . . ."

There was no time. Shannon grabbed Carol by the arm and pulled her out of the room. "Look after my patient, Ella. She's doing fine, but if the dilation isn't complete within the next twenty minutes, we should consider emergency procedures." Shannon was reassured: Ella had already taken charge and was bending solicitously over the hospital bed.

"Ow . . . ." Carol complained as she was dragged through the door. "You'll pay for this, you bitch."

"Henry!" Shannon called out to a passing orderly once they were in the hall and the door was closed behind her. "Take Carol home. And don't let her out."

She thrust the girl into the startled old man's arms and ran up the hallway. She knew it was bad psychology for a doctor to run in a hospital: it alarmed the patients and the staff. But this was an exception. She knew something was dreadfully wrong. An unconscious fear took hold of her heart and she choked back a sob.

Please God, she prayed. *Please let him be all right.*

IT DIDN'T TAKE LONG for Shannon to reach her grandfather's office in the executive suite on the top floor of the hospital. Her grandfather had had the hospital built to his exact specifications only five years before. Although small, it was more modern and more efficient than any other hospital in Egypt. In many ways it was better equipped than the public hospital in Aswan, the only other medical facility in the vicinity.

Urgently, Shannon tapped on the door. "Come in," a woman's voice beckoned.

Shannon took in the scene in the office with one quick glance. Her grandfather was stretched out on the couch, his feet elevated, a light cotton blanket pulled up under his chin. With relief, Shannon realized that he was alive. His face was pale, but his bright eyes immediately turned to greet her.

Shannon knelt beside him and reached for his hand. "Your nails are blue. You've had another attack."

The nurse nodded her head. "Yes. And he wouldn't let me call anyone but you."

Shannon nodded sadly. "Thank you. You can go

now, Beth. But stay close by outside the door in case I need you. And arrange for the emergency equipment, as well."

"No, Shanty . . . don't," her grandfather said in a steady and authoritative voice. There could be no doubt that he knew what he wanted.

"But, grandfather," Shannon protested. "Why?"

"There's no point, that's why. Leave it be. If I'm destined to live, then live I will. But if not, not."

"For me?"

"No. I must have it my way." The way he spoke deliberately and slowly—told Shannon how weak he had become.

Shannon sighed inaudibly. She turned her head toward Beth and nodded for her to go. The door closed quietly behind her. Shannon slumped by the sofa, resting her head on her hands, which were clasped in front of her. She couldn't understand her grandfather's resignation. He was a famous surgeon, and he had devoted his life to a fight against death.

"I know what you are thinking," he said. "But at a certain point acceptance is an act of mercy. But enough of philosophy. You look in worse shape than I do," he commented wryly.

"Was it bad?"

"Can't say it wasn't. Where were you?"

"In the labor room. It was a difficult situation and the nurse was held up getting over to relieve me." Shannon decided not to tell her grandfather about Carol's behavior. He certainly didn't need anything upsetting him right now.

"But I want to know about *you*. How are you feeling now?" Shannon shifted to unbutton his shirt and loosen his tie. "You're not cold, are you?"

It was not at all cool in the room, but a victim of a heart attack could become easily chilled. *Victim*. The word lingered in Shannon's mind. She couldn't imagine her grandfather as a victim of anything, not even old age. She gazed sadly at his handsome, weathered face, etched with the lines of decades. "Wisdom traces," he called them. He was now eighty-four, or so he thought. Accurate records of his birth in San Francisco had never been found. But he knew how old he had been at the time of the earthquake, and since his middle name was August, his birthday had always been celebrated on August first.

"No . . . no, I'm not cold." His deep, gravelly voice broke into her thoughts. His speech betrayed a trembling that had never been there before. His sentences were cut to the minimum to conserve energy.

"Listen," he went on purposefully. "We must talk. I have left everything to you. Papers in my desk. There is a certain sum that goes to Carol next year, when she turns twenty-one."

Shannon nodded; she knew about this. Carol constantly told her that as soon as that money came to her, she would be off like a bird. It was a little inheritance, all that was left of Carol's father's wealth. Roger Blain had died when Carol was a baby, and her beautiful party-loving mother, Lena, had managed to throw most of Roger's money away. It was Shannon's father, a widower himself, and a lawyer who had persuaded Lena to put what remained into a trust fund for her young daughter.

The years of solitude following his own wife's death had made Brendan Mallison extremely susceptible to the lavish attentions of the attractive and bright Lena Blain. He thought they would make a perfect family: two widowed parents, each with a young daughter. So, in his own gentlemanly fashion, he had "persuaded" Lena to marry him; in reality, it was Lena who had contrived the marriage. For a few years, the lawyer's rational lifestyle seemed to have a calming effect on Lena's effervescent personality. But Lena's influence on Brendan was stronger, and her impetuous nature finally proved to be too much for both of them. She convinced her home-loving husband to escort her to one last, wild party and they were killed in a tragic head-on crash in the early hours of the morning, on their way home from the affair.

Carol and Shannon, two very different teenagers with virtually nothing in common, had been united first by marriage and then by death. Their legal guardian was Charles Mallison, Shannon's grandfather, Brendan's father.

Moving from San Francisco to Aswan, Egpyt, was a shock to both girls. Egypt was a mysterious land, offering riches and poverty in equal measure. To Shannon, the move signaled the beginning of an enriching and loving relationship with a grandfather she had heard much but had never really known. Charles Mallison was famous for his brilliant research into bilharzia, a horrifying disease introduced to Egypt with the building of the Aswan High Dam. The virus was spread by the snails which lived in the irrigation canals. With the completion of the dam in 1971, the disease had become rampant, affecting as much as sixty percent of the population. Inspired by her grandfather's dedication and enthusiasm, Shannon, too, had become a doctor, although she had not followed his lead in the choice of specialty. And, although she lacked friends, there were days when the satisfaction of her work was all she needed . . . except for her grandfather, of course.

"Grandfather, we don't need to talk like this. You're strong. Please . . . allow me to help you."

The desperation and sorrow in her voice gave him pause. He knew how much he meant to her. After the deaths of both her mother and her father, she had latched onto Charles as if he were the earth's sole survivor. The fact that he had lived so long comforted her, but he was afraid she had convinced herself that he was immortal, that he would never die.

He had noted her unusual dedication to her profession and to the continual study of current medical knowledge. Her hatred of fatal diseases was extreme. Obstetrics, the one branch of medicine concerned with the renewal, not the end, of life, was the field she liked best, the most optimistic branch of medicine. Death had been too close an enemy for her to live with it day in and day out. Charles Mallison understood; he knew it was hard enough to come to terms with death under the most normal circumstances.

Under her grandfather's tutelage, Shannon had
poured her energy and love into a study of childbirth. Within a year of having received her degree,
she had set up a maternity ward in the hospital unlike
any other in Egypt. In fact, it was starting to come to
the favorable attention of the elite circle of the International Association of Obstetricians. Charles was
proud of his granddaughter. She had already done
very well, and she was only at the beginning of her
life. He had helped her get started, it was true, but
she was on her own now. She didn't need him any
longer.

"Dearest Shanty . . . you will learn to accept my
death. It's time." He paused heavily before continuing. "I wanted to talk to you about something
important. The money I've put into this hospital and
the capital I've put behind it are gone. I'm worried
about the future. We're running out of funds. It's
about time you knew the truth. If the Egyptian
government doesn't come through with some kind of
continuing subsidy, we're going to be in trouble."

"Is it that bad?" Shannon asked, frowning. She
knew there were financial difficulties in running the
hospital, which had been built out of her grandfather's personal fortune, but she had no idea the
situation was as serious as her grandfather indicated.

"I'm afraid so. It's clear we can't go on like this
much longer. I would like to ask you something, and
I want you to think carefully before you answer.
What are you going to do if the government refuses
to give us the support we need?"

"Well, there's always my inheritance. And Carol's, too."

"That wouldn't solve anything. It would deprive you of your inheritance and ease the situation for a couple of years, that's all. Then you would be back where you started. Only this time both you and the hospital would be destitute. No, I'm afraid that's not the answer."

Shannon stood up and walked across the room, a worried expression on her face. "I don't care what it costs. We've got to keep the hospital open, grandfather," she said resolutely, turning to face him. "I intend to do everything in my power to keep your work here alive."

"And what about Carol?"

"Carol is young," Shannon said hurriedly, feeling she had to defend her stepsister. "However, if things get worse, I'm sure she'll be glad to help out in any way she can."

"No time to lie, Shanty," he said gently, looking at her closely. "Face the truth. Carol doesn't care. She never has. She's a selfish young woman."

"Well . . . she wants her freedom and independence, but that doesn't mean . . . ."

"All Carol wants is money. She's not a free spirit. She doesn't know what freedom and independence mean. That only comes with maturity."

"You're not being fair, grandfather. You've got to realize that Carol has been lost and vulnerable since her mother died."

"Her problems have been no different from your

own. You and Carol are different. She's like that mother of hers. She doesn't give a damn about this place, and never has. Don't count on her, Shanty. She won't give you help, financial or otherwise. She would only be a burden."

He moved restlessly and held out a trembling hand to her. "I'm sorry for being so blunt. There isn't much time and I have to tell you the facts."

When Shannon looked down at his pale face, tight with pain and tension, she softened immediately. Her grandfather lapsed into an exhausted silence. Had this outburst against Carol proved to be too much for him? Shannon leaned over him with fear. "Grandfather?" she whispered, first softly and then more loudly.

"You know what the Egyptians would say?" he went on, as if there had been no interruption. "*Malish*—never mind. Who cares, after all? We walk over six centuries of tombs. How could anyone care about a single life? Especially such an old fellow like me. I've had my turn. Death is a natural force."

Shannon could not contain herself any longer. Tears streamed down her face. She jumped to her feet to get a tissue from his desk.

"Oh, I've upset you. I'm sorry," he said slowly, each word carefully enunciated. "I know I can get too philosophical at times. Now . . . to the things of this world. You will have to take over the administration of the hospital. But I wouldn't want you to do it all the time. It would take away from your serious work too much. Also, you'll need to find someone . . . a surgeon. Get the best you can—everything depends on it. And about your work—I think you should consider opening a series of clinics all over Egypt. Then perhaps worldwide. You must reach people . . . that is the only way."

Shannon sat down beside the sofa again. She nodded her head. He had said this to her many times before but she wasn't about to object the way she usually did. Besides, she didn't trust her voice.

"But the most important thing I have to say to you before I go has to do with female things."

His words surprised Shannon. Female things? What exactly did he mean? An expression such as "female things" was not part of her grandfather's vocabulary. Curiosity overcame her emotions. "What do you mean, female things?"

"Now don't get mad. Maybe I've finally gotten old and dotty, but I notice that you don't have many friends, especially those of the male persuasion. . . ."

"Grandfather!"

"Now just listen. Don't forget that people on their deathbed have certain rights," he said with a smile that betrayed his sense of humor. "One's work *is* important, it's true. But it is more important to love. I can't tell you the sweetness of my memories of Lydia, your grandmother. You know, Shanty, ours is an atheistic profession. We tend to look at human beings like machines, and their parts seem like nuts and bolts. But I think there might be more. I wonder if there is an afterlife. I wonder if I might be with Lydia again. . . ."

He closed his eyes and dozed for a second, a tender smile on his lips. Shannon rested her head against his chest, comforted by the faint yet persistent heartbeat within.

"Oh, but I'm wandering," he said with a start, his eyes open. "What was I talking about?"

"Love," Shannon reminded him with a smile.

"Of course . . . love. And men," he added with a feeble wink. "You know, Dr. Jason Wilfred seems to think a lot of you."

"Grandfather, how would you know?"

Shannon and Jason had been dating and Jason had proved attentive, but Shannon hadn't felt that their relationship would ever be anything more than casual.

"Oh, you can't pull the wool over my eyes, young woman. I don't know him very well, but I did know his mother and father. He's only been with us a few months, but he seems okay. If you were to . . . you know . . . I'd rest easy, I think. And just think how educational it would be for you to study obstetrics from the other side. . . ."

"Is that your idea of a joke?"

"Well, I had intended it to be. But I guess it came out badly. Remember, deathbed rights, you know. I'm allowed to make bad and distasteful jokes. I can even be downright silly if I want to," he said smugly.

"Oh, grandfather, you old horse. Nothing's going to kill you. Look at you! Your color is back, you can talk a blue streak. If you don't mind some professional advice, I would suggest that you get up off that deathbed you're so fond of and we'll take you to my house, where you'll at least be more comfortable." With a wince Shannon remembered Carol. The last thing her grandfather needed was to see Carol in her present condition.

"Better yet," she added with a false, bright voice. "why don't we move you into one of your very own hospital beds?"

"A private room?"

"Nothing but. How about the deluxe suite?"

"Well, okay," he said grudgingly. "It is kind of embarrassing, I have to confess, to gear all up for death and then be stood up."

Shannon laughed and shook her head. How could anyone not love such a man? "You're nothing but an old fool. What were your last words going to be, anyway? Had you rehearsed them?" she asked playfully, kissing him on the cheek and helping him to his feet.

"Shanty! How could you say such a thing?" He chuckled. "But it's not a bad idea . . . now that you mention it."

Chapter 2

Shannon never saw her grandfather alive again. At dawn the following morning, Dr. Charles Mallison suffered a massive heart attack and died instantly. Shannon was completely devastated. Never in her life had she felt so completely and utterly alone. After the death of her father, she had clung to her grandfather as the one strong being who would live to comfort her. In mourning the loss of her grandfather, she felt the overwhelming pain of having lost both her mother and father. Orphaned for the third time, she wondered how she would ever be able to carry on.

Automatically, she had turned to Jason, whose affection and tender words of encouragement had carried her through a painful and difficult period. The days passed in a haze of pain.

Finally, she realized she had to take the situation in

hand. She decided to take her grandfather's advice and announce to the senior staff members her decision to take over the administration of the hospital. She was well aware of the enormity of the task facing her—the long hours of hard work, the daily problems that would have to be met and resolved. But she was determined to see her grandfather's work continued.

She arranged, one afternoon, to see the heads of the various departments. They all gathered in her office for their first official meeting with the new head of the Mallison Hospital.

Shannon cast a quick glance at Jason, who smiled reassuringly, and then looked over at Carol, who was casually lighting a cigarette. The indifferent expression on Carol's face made it obvious she wasn't the least bit interested in the proceedings.

Shannon turned to her audience, took a deep breath and began. "The reason I've asked you all here today is to tell you I'll be taking my grandfather's place as administrator of the hospital."

Her announcement was greeted by a murmur of approval. She thanked the staff with a grateful smile and continued.

"I know it's going to be difficult for me, but I'm determined to carry on my grandfather's work to the best of my abilities. I'm well aware of the difficulties that lie ahead, and I realize I don't have the high degree of knowledge or experience my grandfather showed. I'm counting on all of you to help me.

"Now—I think you should all realize that our

financial situation is not good. We will have to work very hard and pull together if we're going to carry on the work that was so close to my grandfather's heart. Seeing you all here like this is very reassuring and I'm confident that I can count on your continuing support."

With a deep sense of relief, Shannon looked gratefully at the faces in front of her. Her audience was beaming with approval and respect. Only Carol remained indifferent and seemingly unmoved by her words.

As Shannon turned and looked at her grandfather's empty chair, her chest constricted and, for a moment, she couldn't go on. She pulled herself together and continued.

"We desperately need another surgeon. It's essential that I find someone to replace my grandfather as soon as possible. When I do, I'll let you know all the details. Until then, we'll continue to send our emergency cases to the public hospital in Aswan.

"I guess that's all for now. I can't think of anything else to say at the moment. Thank you all for coming and keep up the good work."

When the meeting broke up, Carol was the first to leave the office. The others slowly drifted out behind her. Only Jason stayed behind. When they were alone, he walked over to Shannon and took her hand in his.

"A little brief but very much to the point. Well done," he said.

"I'm not very good at that kind of thing," Shannon

replied. "I don't know what happened to me. It was stupid really. I couldn't make the speech I'd prepared. I don't know what it is, but I don't seem to be cut out for making speeches."

"Don't worry about it," Jason replied quickly. "You said what had to be said and got right down to basics. You communicated the essential points. That's what counts," he added reassuringly.

"Jason, before I tell the others, I want to ask your advice about my grandfather's possible replacement."

"Do you have someone in mind?"

"Yes, I do. He's from France."

"I kind of thought you would choose an American."

"I was thinking of that. But, I was looking through a medical journal, and I saw this advertisement," she replied, handing him the magazine.

Jason took the magazine from her outstretched hand and began reading the announcement she had circled in red.

Surgeon seeking employment abroad. Previous experience; Balorial Hospital, Paris, and well-known private clinic in Neuilly. Please send replies care of this journal. All mail will be forwarded.

"I didn't tell you about this before because I wanted to wait until I had more information about him. I answered the ad and here's the reply I got this morning," Shannon explained, as she handed Jason a letter and two other documents.

Dear Dr. Mallison:

   In response to your letter, I enclose herewith photocopies of my references and hope they will be satisfactory. I would be delighted to live and work in Aswan and find the financial remuneration for the position adequate.

   I would like to make it quite clear that my reasons for leaving the Iris Clinic are strictly personal and in no way involve my professional life or competence as a surgeon.

   I look forward to hearing from you at your earliest possible convenience.

                                   Yours sincerely,
                                   Cliff Sinclair

His references were excellent and obviously authentic; they came from the well-known head of the Bichat Hospital in Paris and from Professor Langet, who was chief of staff at the Sydney Clinic in London. The first reference stated that Doctor Cliff Sinclair, resident surgeon, Bichat Hospital, had acted as assistant to Professor Maillant, who was famous for his brilliant surgical work both in France and abroad. It went on to explain that, much to the regret of his colleagues and supervisors, Dr. Sinclair had left Bichat to take over as head of surgery in a famous private clinic at Neuilly.

The second reference confirmed these facts and went on to state that Dr. Cliff Sinclair had worked at the Iris Clinic for eighteen months. It also noted that, in that time, Dr. Sinclair had made notable scientific advances and had drawn a great deal of praise from the medical community at large for his work at the clinic in the field of transplant surgery.

"Well, what do you think?" Shannon asked.

"If these references are anything to go by, he's a good catch. Transplant surgery . . . Dr. Sinclair . . . I've heard of him. Yes—remember, a year or so ago, wasn't he in the news?"

"Yes! I do remember now. Why would he want to work for us, I wonder. Well, nevertheless, I want to hire him."

"Why not? You're the boss now," Jason replied. "My dear chief of staff," he added, as he walked toward her and lightly brushed her lips with his. "I hope your new duties won't keep you from spending a few minutes with me every now and then."

"Oh, I think I can swing it," she replied glibly.

"I insist on it," he stated calmly, as he pulled her to him and looked into her gray eyes.

"Please be patient a little longer, Jason," she said softly, as she disengaged herself from his embrace.

"But why?" he asked impatiently. He stood apart from her, his hands aggressively set on his hips. He was about her height, but stockier. Sometimes, because of his dimple, hazel eyes and his headful of curly brown hair, Shannon thought he looked like an adorable teddy bear. "Aren't you sure about me?"

Jason asked. "Sometimes you feel so far away, so withdrawn. I can't help wondering what you're thinking about at those times."

"I know I've been preoccupied lately, Jason, but I've had a lot on my mind. I'm sorry, darling, really I am. But please try to understand. I'm worried about the hospital. I don't know how we're going to survive without that subsidy from the government. And the whole idea of being head of the Foundation is very new to me and quite overwhelming. There's so much to deal with—so much to think about. But things will be better soon, I promise. Just be patient, all right? You've been such a great help to me, Jason, and I'm thankful."

"Well, can we at least have dinner tonight?" he asked.

They rarely had the chance to go out together. And, when they did want to be alone, they had gone far from the hospital to avoid annoying gossip.

"The White Nile?" He pressed.

"It's too close, Jason. We're sure to run into some-one from the hospital and tomorrow, everyone would be talking about us."

"So what? Who cares if someone sees us? We're free to go out with whomever we please. And besides, it's time people knew. All this secrecy doesn't make any sense."

Shannon's attitude annoyed him. He couldn't understand why she didn't want people to know they were seeing each other. However, he refused to discuss the matter any further.

"I'll wait for you down by the felucca dock. I'll see you there at six o'clock."

Determined to avoid an argument, Shannon didn't press her point, and after a momentary hesitation, she smiled and accepted his invitation.

"Great! We'll make a romantic evening of it," he said, as he walked toward the door. "Oh, by the way, since you've decided to hire Sinclair, you'd better write to him right away. We need a surgeon here as soon as possible."

"Right. I'll draw up a contract immediately and send it to him in the afternoon mail," she said, nodding quickly.

He held her gaze for a long moment. Slowly, he turned and left the office.

Feeling tired to her bones, Shannon slumped down in her office chair. Her confusion about the attention Jason was paying her only added to her emotional burdens. She had asked herself over and over, but she honestly didn't know how she felt about him.

AT THE END OF THE AFTERNOON, when Shannon stepped outside the hospital, the blazing heat of the Egyptian June day hit her with full force. For two weeks now, every time she left the house or the hospital, she had felt as if she were walking into an inferno. Even though it was five o'clock in the evening and the sun was setting, the air was still dry and burning. At this time of day the temperature had gone down somewhat, but it was still unbearably hot. There wasn't a breath of air anywhere, not even a hint of a cool breeze. In the little garden enclosed by the white hospital walls, which glistened in the late afternoon sun, the long, slim leaves of the eucalyptus trees and the dark green briar bushes stood spellbound in the one hundred-degree heat. Even the shade offered no relief.

Ignoring the gardener, who was listlessly watering the hibiscus plants and other brightly colored flowers that were withering in the implacable heat of the Egyptian sun, Shannon hurried toward the little group of houses that stood on the far edge of the hospital property overlooking the Nile. The houses were small but comfortable and housed members of the hospital staff. The first three were occupied by senior female personnel. Jason and Dr. Bechir Hinawi lived in the fourth one and the fifth, which now stood empty, had belonged to her grandfather.

Shannon walked quickly toward the first house, which she shared with Carol. It was just big enough for their needs. It had a small foyer, a kitchen, bathroom, living room and two bedrooms. When she walked in the front door, she was greeted by a rush of cool air from the air-conditioning unit. The shades were drawn, and the cool, dim interior was a welcome relief from the blazing white heat outside.

Shannon usually arrived home from the hospital at this time. As always, when she walked in the door, the house immediately came to life. Nadah, the young Nubian servant, began chattering and Pepsie, Shannon's little tabby with the triangular head, so common in the cats of ancient Egypt, began to meow and purr happily. Even Ozir, the blue parakeet who had been sleeping on his perch, began fluttering around, singing and clattering the chain of his cage. Carol was the only one who didn't respond to Shannon's arrival. She often just sat motionless, a cigarette in one hand, a drink in the other. Today she was nowhere in sight.

Nadah came running along the tiled floor in bare feet to greet her.

"Don't go into the bathroom," she warned Shannon. "There's a big scorpion in there. I can't imagine how it got in. I asked Yassef to come and kill it," she added.

"Couldn't you kill it?" Shannon asked in surprise.

"I was afraid he might sting me. He's as big as my hand, and he moves really fast."

As Shannon passed the bathroom, she looked in to see if she could get a glimpse of the scorpion. It wasn't as big as Nadah had described it. Standing motionless against the wall behind the sink, it seemed to be waiting for an invisible adversary. Its front legs, tapering off into small claws, and the trunk of its body and long stinger lay flat on the tiled floor. If she hadn't been wearing thin-soled sandals, she would have gone in and killed the thing herself, she thought. But the idea made her shudder.

"One day before you came to Aswan, a gardener got stung by one of those things," Nadah said, coming up behind her. "His leg swelled right up and turned all black. If Dr. Hinawi hadn't taken care of him right away, he would have died for sure," she added as she closed the bathroom door carefully behind her.

Shannon knew that the venom from certain

scorpions was lethal—many people had died from their deadly poison.

"Tell me when Yassef gets here, will you?" she asked as she went into her bedroom. "I want to take a shower."

She opened the curtains to let in some light but kept the window closed against the heat. The view from her room was magnificent. Aswan was a city of more than two hundred thousand, stretched out along the shores of the Nile. The bay window of her room faced east and looked out over the Nile where Elephant Island, so named because of huge, dark-gray rocks, rose majestically out of the clear blue waters. A small felucca with a patchwork sail was gliding slowly down the river, and on the far shore the palace of the Aga Khan stood gracefully on a little hill, a brilliant white against the deep blue sky.

The Foundation had been built on the edge of the city and from where she stood, Shannon could see the neighborhood next to the compound—a village in itself with its roofless little shacks and dusty roads where children played noisily. She knew the sound of their happy shouts piercing the hot dry air, mingling with the bleating of the goats and the constant hum of the endless conversations of the men sitting huddled in the shade in small groups, discussing everything from the price of tobacco to the state of the nation.

As she stood there looking out at the little village, Shannon spotted an old woman dressed in black walking along the dirt road. In keeping with the local custom, she was draped from head to toe in the traditional veils. A mangy-looking sandy colored dog was straggling along at her heels as she made her way down to the river, an earthenware jar firmly balanced on her head. Each day she followed the same ritual. She would go down to the water, fill her jar, wash her face and then head for home.

In the early morning and late evening, Shannon often stood at her window and watched life unfold in the little sunbaked village that seemed to thrive in the blazing heat of the African sun. Until now, the village had been just a moving tableau of sights and sounds. But tonight it was different. As the heat of the day began to ease, and she opened the window to let in the cool, evening air, everything suddenly became real and alive. The sounds from the little village came right into her room. The shrill voices of the women, the children's laughter, the dogs barking and fighting over meager scraps of food, the braying of a donkey, the strange haunting strains of Arab music, all took on the vividness of real life.

Before long, the sound of voices from inside the house distracted her from her meditations. In the distance she could hear Yassef's deep baritone voice and Nadah's high-pitched laughter. Yassef was the general handyman around the hospital and had worked there ever since it had been built. He was devoted to Shannon. He did everything around the place; fixed the plumbing, replaced burned-out fuses and chauffeured people around town. Over the years, his help had become indispensable.

When he left, Nadah came to tell Shannon it was safe to use the bathroom. Shannon undressed quickly and slipped into her bathrobe. She was a tall, lithe woman and the shapeless white doctor's coat she wore at the hospital disguised her grace and slender beauty. Although she was twenty-five, she had the figure of a seventeen-year-old. She pulled out the numerous hairpins that held her bun in place and shook her head with pleasure, feeling her thick, wavy blond hair cascading down her back. It was getting very long—soon it would reach her waist.

A moment later she was in the shower, luxuriating in the cool water that sprayed down over her tired, hot body. For a long time, she stood motionless under the shower jet and let her mind go completely blank. When she was totally refreshed, she went back to her room and lay down on her bed. It had been another long day.

WHEN SHE GOT HOME, Carol immediately slipped into some lightweight slacks and a cotton top and brushed her hair. Then she walked down the hall to the dining room. Nadah had opened the window and removed the mosquito netting to let the cool, evening air from the nearby river flood into the room.

From his perch in his cage, Ozir threw an indifferent look at Carol as she entered the room. Silently, with his nose in the air, he turned his back on her.

Carol poured herself a whiskey and sat down in a big comfortable armchair, aware of the sound of dishes clattering as Nadah prepared supper in the kitchen.

When Shannon came into the dining room wearing a beautiful gown, Carol realized her stepsister was going out for the evening with Jason.

"Do you want a drink?" she asked mechanically.

"Just some mango juice, please."

A polite indifference reigned as Carol pushed aside the hibiscus flowers Nadah always placed on the supper table and picked up the glass pitcher.

"I don't suppose you're all dressed up on my account," Carol remarked dryly, as she handed Shannon a glass.

"I won't be having dinner here this evening," Shannon replied.

"Are you going out with Jason Wilfred?"

"Yes, I am," Shannon replied somewhat unwillingly. "We have some important matters to discuss."

"Business?" Carol asked, smiling ironically.

Shannon set her glass down on the table and walked over to the parakeet, who was fluttering around on his perch.

"Yes, business," she replied wearily, as she scratched the bird's head with her index finger.

"You still don't want to admit that you're dating, do you?" commented Carol, grinning broadly. "I talked with Jason this afternoon, you know. I told him how stupid I thought you both were."

Shannon turned to face her stepsister. "Where did you see him?"

"Didn't he tell you?"

"We didn't get much chance to talk all day. We were both too busy."

"I suppose you're just dying to know what we talked about." Carol smirked.

"Not really," Shannon replied calmly.

"Oh, yes, you are. I can tell by the look in your eyes," she continued slowly, as she sat motionless at the table, watching the older woman like a hawk. "Well, you don't have to worry. The good doctor Wilfred just isn't my type and I'm certainly not his."

"Carol, what are you trying to prove? Or are you making trouble for the fun of it?" Shannon stalked back to the table and picked up her glass. She took a sip of juice, put the glass on the table and then walked out of the room.

When the door closed behind her stepsister, Carol picked up a purple hibiscus flower from the table and began tearing it to shreds. "Have a nice evening, Shannon," she muttered between clenched teeth.

IT WAS A CLEAR, starry night. Shannon went down to the river to meet Jason, who was waiting for her a little way past the dock where the feluccas were moored. At this hour of the evening, the place was very busy. Even though June wasn't the best time to visit Egypt, there were loads of tourists in Aswan, and tonight it seemed that most of them were down at the docks, hiring feluccas to take them across the river to where the multicolored lights of a well-known restaurant shone brightly against the night sky.

As soon as he saw her, Jason walked over and took her hands in his. "Shannon, you look great. Come on, let's get on that boat the tourists have rented."

She smiled, and together they boarded the small felucca with its two-man Egyptian crew. As the boat glided in between the huge rocks of Elephant Island, whose monstrous shapes loomed up in the pale moonlight, Shannon and Jason sat side by side, neither saying a word. On all sides there was the happy chatter of the tourists, excited and ready for a night on the town.

In a few minutes they reached the other side of the river, which was brilliantly lit by the lights from the restaurant. A pathway, bordered with brightly colored flowers, led to a massive stairway that climbed straight up the sheer rock to the White Nile restaurant, situated in a grove of tall, stately trees overlooking the river.

A vast foyer opened out onto a big circular room with an earthen floor. Small, round tables, covered with red tablecloths, and chairs of dark leather were arranged in the dim, intimate lighting. Waiters wearing either white jackets or long, traditional robes with voluminous sleeves showed guests to their tables as they arrived. One of them led Jason and Shannon to a table near the stage where a troup of Nubian dancers would perform later in the evening.

When they were seated, they ordered some tangy Egyptian beer and made a few selections from the many main dishes and hors d'oeuvres the place was famous for.

"Alone at last," Jason said, smiling slightly as he looked around the crowded restaurant.

When Shannon caught Jason's eye, she motioned discreetly to a couple sitting at a table beside some

German tourists. Jason had never seen the woman before and didn't quite know what Shannon was trying to tell him.

"Didn't I tell you we would run into people we know?" she said with a worried look.

"Why, that's Bechir Hinawi," Jason exclaimed, as he recognized his colleague from the hospital. "I heard he was going to marry a girl from a highly respected Egyptian family. He certainly has good taste. She's beautiful."

Shannon didn't say a word and Jason immediately realized she was feeling awkward and ill-at-ease.

"I know their presence here bothers you, Shannon," he said, taking her hand in his. "But don't let it get to you. Try to forget they're here. Enjoy yourself. Let's put the cares of the hospital behind us for one night and just have a good time. Come on, what do you say? We both deserve it."

Shannon nodded silently and tried to ignore the dark, inquisitive gaze of the Egyptian doctor who was sitting at the nearby table.

The waiter brought a bottle of champagne and uncorked it with a flourish.

"Champagne?" Shannon asked. "Why?"

"Well . . . I was going to wait for a more favorable mood, but I might as well tell you now." Jason poured the bubbling mixture. He lifted his glass, tipping it to touch hers. "To you . . . and to me."

Shannon smiled and took a sip. "You're sweet and very thoughtful. Thank you," she said.

"Forgive me for being blunt, Shannon. But that's the type of person I am. I won't beat about the bush. I think we should get married."

Shannon was completely taken aback. She hadn't given marriage any thought. She sat there tongue-tied, thinking feverishly. Jason was sweet, and he had been patient and supportive. He was a good person, and she respected him as a doctor, too. But was this love? She wondered if it could be; she wondered if love might grow.

Jason noticed her hesitation.

She smiled and reached gratefully for his hand. "Thank you. I'm flattered. It's just that I never expected . . . that is, I never thought . . . I'm sorry, I don't know what to say." She blushed, quite beside herself with the unaccustomed emotions.

She looked across the table at Jason. He was a nice-looking man, she thought. Not handsome, but nice-looking, nevertheless. His round face was flushed with emotion and when he smiled tentatively at her, the charming dimple in his right cheek showed. His curly brown hair and hazel eyes always evoked a trusting response in her. Although she had never met his parents, her grandfather had known them rather well, and had good things to say about them. She remembered, briefly, her grandfather's wish that she marry Jason. Her grandfather's advice had always been good before. Was he right when it came to matters of the heart? How would she ever know?

"Say yes, please, Shannon. I promise you'll never regret it." Jason pulled a small jeweler's box out of his pocket and opened it. A dazzling diamond sparkled in a beautiful, antique Tiffany setting. "It's all yours . . . just say the word."

"Jason . . . ."

Jason looked at Shannon expectantly, eagerly.

"I want to think it over," Shannon whispered, almost too confused to speak.

"Please, Shannon, no. I couldn't bear it! Say yes . . . just say yes. You know I'll make you happy. I promise you I will. Do you want me to get down on my knees?" he asked, a hint of distress in his voice.

"Okay . . . yes, then, I say yes," Shannon burst in a rush of words, her face flushed with confusion.

"Shannon!" Jason whispered and reached for her hands. "Put the ring on now . . . will you? I want to see how it fits."

"Not here," Shannon said uneasily, glancing at the tables around them. "I just ask one thing . . . that this be kept a secret until everything settles down and returns to normal. It wouldn't be kind to the memory of my grandfather to announce such a thing at this time, don't you agree?"

"Well, no, I don't agree with you, but—I'll go along with it, for your sake."

At that moment, the waiter appeared at their table with several small cups of sauce, a bowl of rice and bean pâté, and a plate of assorted meats. When he was finished serving them, he bowed and left.

"Would you like to start off with a brochette?" Jason asked.

Before Shannon could answer, Jason was suddenly distracted by a curvaceous figure dressed in a clinging, revealing dress, standing at the top of the staircase that led up from the river.

Chapter 3

"It's Carol!" Jason exclaimed in amazement.

Shannon shuddered but didn't say a word.

"Did you tell her we were coming here?" Jason asked, turning to look at her in surprise.

Shannon shook her head wordlessly, realizing she'd almost asked the same question.

Looking relaxed and poised, Carol remained standing at the top of the stairway and slowly surveyed the crowded restaurant below. Not a few admiring men turned openly to view her. She completely ignored Shannon and Jason and said a few words to one of the waiters, who proceeded to lead her to a table that faced the entrance of the restaurant. At that moment, several men's voices called out to her over the hum of conversation.

"Carol," they cried excitedly.

A young man with long fair hair and a neatly

trimmed beard, who sat at a table with three other men, was desperately trying to get her attention.

Carol whirled around and stared blankly in his direction. Her face brightened with recognition and they exchanged a few words. Then she nodded when he pointed to an empty chair at their table. Carol accepted his invitation eagerly.

Shannon and Jason had watched the little scene from their vantage point nearby. They were too far away to hear what was being said, but they had seen enough to get the general idea.

The young man turned to the waiter and asked him to set an extra place. Then, turning to one of the three other men at his table, he made the introductions. The group burst into laughter and conversation.

"Let's eat, shall we?" Shannon suggested suddenly, avoiding any comment on what they had both witnessed. "And yes, I would like to begin with a brochette," she added.

As Shannon began to eat, the insistent rhythm of a tambourine announced the appearance of the Nubian dancers on stage. With their black skin glistening in the bright lights, in sharp contrast to their long, white, traditional costumes, they began to interpret the ancient dances of their country. As they stamped their feet on the hard, earthen floor, their agile, sinuous bodies twisted and turned to the rhythm of the music.

"You're not sorry you came, are you?" Jason asked.

Shannon looked over at him and smiled. All she had wanted was a quiet, peaceful evening. "If I can just forget Carol is here, I'll be fine," she sighed.

Five musicians were on stage now, sitting behind the dancers, playing the strange, haunting music that floated out over the noisy hum of conversation in the crowded restaurant. As they watched the intricate moves of the Nubian dancers, Jason and Shannon slowly ate the food they had ordered.

Most people were too interested in the performance to talk. Once the dancers left the stage and the waiters began serving fruit and trays of Egyptian pastries, conversation began again. It was getting late. There was a lot of laughing now, especially at Carol's table, where the three men seemed to be in high spirits and enjoying the company of their guest. The restaurant seemed infected with a feeling of frantic gaiety that was a little too noisy for Shannon's taste.

Every now and then, Carol's laugh rang out in cascades of silvery sound over the other voices. Shannon did her best to ignore her stepsister and continued to eat the ripe mango Jason had picked out for her, intent on savoring the delicious flavor to the full.

From where he was sitting, Jason had a clear view of Carol's table. The little group was loudly applauding Carol and the young man, who had downed their beers in one long swallow. They were obviously having a good time sampling the sweet Egyptian pastries, some of which were stuffed with an exotic almond paste and covered in a sticky sauce that left everyone very thirsty. There were continual requests for beer and wine from the group at Carol's table.

Shannon was determined to ignore what her stepsister was doing and resolutely turned the conversation to business. "I drew up the contract for Cliff Sinclair and sent Yassef to mail it for me. It's too bad we're in such a hurry for a surgeon. If we'd had more time, we could have checked up on him more thoroughly."

"Weren't you satisfied with his references?"

"The references were fine. It's just that we don't know anything about him. Why would he want to come to such an out-of-the-way hospital as ours? I did a little bit of research. He's world famous. One year he was even nominated for a Nobel prize. It doesn't make sense. We don't know anything—his family situation, his background, how old he is, that kind of thing."

"Is it the man or the surgeon you're hiring?"

"Well, a surgeon is a man first, isn't he?"

"There's a profound thought," Jason teased, a twinkle in his eye.

"Okay, make fun of me if you like," she said calmly. "But what if Dr. Sinclair shows up here with a wife and half a dozen kids? What will we do then? Our living accommodations are limited—we wouldn't have room for a big family."

"If Sinclair were married with a family, he would have told you."

"There wasn't time for anything but the briefest of telegrams; everything happened so quickly. Anyway, we'll know more about him soon enough. I asked him to answer right away, and he's going to send a telegram with the date and time of his arrival."

The musicians and dancers had returned to the stage and, as Shannon turned to watch them, Jason observed Carol out of the corner of his eyes. Her dress was a shiny, bright red that jarred with the red of her hair. The plunging neckline drew attention to her plump breasts. Like fruits being served on a platter, he thought. When he noted her overly bright eyes and her flushed cheeks, he realized how much she had had to drink.

Shannon noticed that Jason's eyes kept straying in Carol's direction. "Carol told me she'd seen you today," Shannon said, determined not to hide anything from him.

"Yes," Jason answered abruptly. "We had quite an interesting little chat," he added, after a brief pause. "Did she tell you what we talked about?"

"No, she only mentioned the conversation—she didn't go into detail. Was it important?"

"Not really. But in the course of the conversation, I saw a side of her I'd never seen before. I don't know what she wanted to say or what she was after, though," Jason replied. "She's full of all kinds of feelings. You and she are so different. It's amazing."

"You're right, we don't have much in common," Shannon admitted slowly, reluctant to enter into a discussion about her stepsister. "And there's not much love lost between us, either," she added bitterly.

"Why is that?"

"Oh, I suppose it's always been like that. We were strangers, thrown together when we came here. And then grandfather and I really got along—I've always wondered how that made Carol feel. And Carol was used to getting all the money she wanted from her mother, and then grandfather started refusing to give her any. I don't suppose that helped matters much. He was putting her share of the inheritance into a special fund 'for a good purpose,' he would say. What he meant was university or college, of course, and Carol would have none of it. She saw me getting money for medical school and she felt she had the right to just as much money for traveling. She tried to convince grandfather of that—he'd never go for it! So she managed to convince herself that it was all my fault. I guess I was easier to pick on than he was.

"But this is all just guessing. We're very different— and we have never been close. It's as simple as that," Shannon said with a shrug. "She's the pretty one; I'm the brainy one."

When Shannon looked up at the performers, she saw one of the male dancers leave the group and walk toward Carol's table. She knew one of the customs at the White Nile: every evening, the major dancer of the troup chose a young woman in the audience for his partner. The evening would end with a high-spirited free-form dance where the professional dancers and the tourists kicked up their heels together in wild abandon.

At first, Carol was reluctant to join the dance but, encouraged by her friends, she finally got up on the stage with the young male dancer and began imitating his sensuous movements. Almost immediately she picked up the rhythm of the music and the sense of the dance, and laughingly followed the intricate steps with surprising ease. As supple as a reed, she bent and swayed with her partner as he executed the complicated steps, her revealing dress and movements as enticing as a professional's. With her curly red hair shining in the bright lights and her bare feet hardly touching the ground, she seemed to cast a spell over the audience that was already hypnotized by the strange, primitive Egyptian music. Gradually, everyone in the room was caught up in the sensuous rhythm, and they began clapping wildly in time to the music.

When the dance ended, everyone burst into enthusiastic applause and cheers. A little overcome, but radiant, Carol ran back to the table and downed a glass of wine. Then she grabbed the tall, blond young man by the hand and led him up to the stage where they started dancing the farandole, a lively peasant dance that ended in a serpentine chain.

In one swift glance, Shannon took in the situation and knew immediately how the evening was going to end for Carol and her handsome young dancing partner.

"Do you want to go now?" Jason asked, sensing her discomfort.

"No, I'm fine," she replied quietly. "Let's stay."

They made desultory small talk, but Shannon's

attention was riveted on her stepsister. At one point their eyes met and from a distance they took stock of one another. In Shannon's eyes there was a look of intense disapproval; in Carol's, open defiance.

Once the dance was over, the dancers went back to their table where Carol proceeded to drink glass after glass of wine. Before long, it became increasingly obvious that the alcohol was beginning to take effect. On the other side of the stage, Dr. Hinawi and his fiancée studiously avoided looking over at Carol's table out of respect for Shannon.

"Carol's had far too much wine," Shannon commented uneasily, feeling she couldn't take much more of the tension. "Any minute now she's going to lose all control and make a spectacle of herself. I'm sorry to ask you this, Jason, but could you go and get her? I think we should take her home. I'd go over, but I know she would never listen to me."

Jason immediately got up and went over to Carol's table. "We're going now, Carol," he said, putting a hand on her bare shoulder. "And we want you to come with us," he added, smiling apologetically to the other men at the table.

"Why, Dr. Jason Wilfred, how nice to see you. Are you doing the dirty work tonight?" she asked innocently, her lips pouted, her green eyes clouded from the effects of the alcohol. "See, I followed your advice. I've made friends my own age and I'm having a terrific time. All my boredom is gone, just like that," she added, snapping her fingers. "I'm having fun—a real blast. But let me introduce you. This is my friend Mark Lorenz, and three of his friends.

Jason is a *very* close friend of my sister's," she continued, as she introduced him to the rest of her party. "My sister watches over me like an old mother hen. I can't tell you how secure that makes me feel," she added sarcastically.

"Shannon is waiting, Carol. Let's go," he said, ignoring her thinly veiled barb.

"I don't want to go home right now. For once, I'm having a good time in this godforsaken place and I don't intend to stop now. Mark can take me home later."

"If you want to remember what you did tonight, I suggest you come home with us right now."

"I don't give a damn what you suggest," she retorted angrily.

"Do you agree, Mark?" Jason asked Mark.

"He's probably right, Carol," Mark replied. "It might be a good idea for you to go home."

Realizing she couldn't fight both of them, Carol decided to give in and go. But she refused to admit total defeat. "All right, then. I'll go. But not because Shannon wants me to. It looks like you're going to have to help me, Dr. Wilfred," she added. "The room seems to be spinning."

After saying goodbye to everyone at her table, she reminded Mark to look her up when he was in town.

"That's a promise," he replied. "As a matter of fact, I'll be back in about two weeks. So I'll see you then, okay?"

Before Carol had a chance to answer Jason took her arm and led her toward the stairway where Shannon was waiting.

"Oh, I feel so dizzy," Carol squealed, ignoring Shannon completely. "I must have eaten too much of that pastry."

"And maybe just a drop too much to drink," Jason answered. Following behind Shannon, he managed to get Carol down the steep stairway to the dock and onto a boat.

During the crossing, Shannon didn't say a word. Carol chattered on happily, seemingly unaware of her sister's stony silence. "Mark Lorenz is a great guy. Too bad there aren't more men like him around here. Why didn't you just leave me alone? I was having such a good time. I wasn't bothering anyone."

She kept up a steady monologue until they reached the front door of the house.

"Would you like to escort me to my bedroom, doctor?" she asked, smiling seductively as she threw a sly, sidelong glance at Shannon. "At the risk of making my stepsister insanely jealous, I just want you to know that I would be absolutely delighted if you undressed me and put me to bed."

Before Carol knew what was happening, Shannon had raised her hand and slapped her across the face. The sound rang loud and sharp in the still night air, and Carol stumbled backward, her hand raised to her face where the mark of Shannon's hand stood out against her pale face. Carol was as white as a sheet and was trembling violently from head to toe. She didn't say a word, but just stared at her stepsister in shocked amazement.

Stunned by Shannon's reaction, Jason whirled

around to face his fiancée. She was shaking with barely concealed anger, her face pale in the moonlight.

Then Carol's voice broke the ringing silence. "You'll pay for that, Shannon. Maybe not now. Maybe not for a long time. But someday, you'll pay for that, I swear it," Carol said dully, her eyes blazing with suppressed rage. She turned on her heel and walked into the house, slamming the door behind her.

"I shouldn't have done that," Shannon said, voice trembling, tears streaming down her cheeks. "So much has been happening. . . . I'm so on edge. . . . I don't know what to do. Carol is driving me crazy. She spoiled my evening . . . and that remark was just the last straw."

Shannon burst into sobs. Jason pulled her into the shadows and took her in his arms. "There was no need to get so upset. Carol didn't mean what she said. She's tired and she's had far too much to drink. Forget it, Shannon. It's not important."

"It wasn't just a harmless remark, Jason. That was her way of getting back at me. She wanted to hurt me and make me jealous."

"But you don't have any reason to be jealous. She was just talking nonsense. If anything, you should feel pity or contempt for the girl. She's pretty mixed up, you know."

"You don't know her like I do," Shannon said wearily. "But anyway, I had no right to slap her. It only made things worse than they already are."

"Don't you think you're overreacting? Listen, Shannon, you're tired. Things will look different in the morning after you've had a good night's sleep," Jason reassured her.

Shannon didn't say a word but, in her heart, she knew he was wrong. "Good night," she said wearily. "I'm sorry. I'm upset and very tired. I think I'll do what you suggest and go to bed."

She kissed him briefly and half stepped through the doorway. Then she turned to wave at him, remembering that this was the man she had promised to marry only hours before.

Chapter 4

Doctor Sinclair's telegram arrived. It was brief and to the point: he would be arriving on the twenty-sixth by the morning plane.

The morning Dr. Sinclair was due, Shannon sent Yassef to the airport to meet him. "When you get back to the hospital, Yassef, bring the doctor straight to my office. I'll be waiting for him there," she informed him.

After a visit to the maternity ward, Shannon returned to her office. She spent most of her time there these days, trying to resolve the administrative difficulties of the hospital.

She was impatient to meet the man who would be replacing her grandfather, and was preparing herself when Yassef entered to announce that Dr. Sinclair was waiting to see her.

"Have him come in," she said quietly.

"The doctor didn't come alone," Yassef said quickly.

When Shannon looked up at him in surprise, he added, "A lady came with him."

"A lady?"

"Yes. She has a lot of luggage with her, too."

Shannon frowned. This is what she had feared. Why hadn't Sinclair mentioned it? True, their correspondence was entirely brief and she had never asked, but . . . . She frowned with frustration. What was she going to do about it?

"Have him come alone," she said, determined not to confront anyone but the surgeon she had hired.

Yassef turned and disappeared into the outer office.

Shannon nervously arranged her hair and checked her clothes. There was no need—she knew she looked presentable. But too much time was going by and there was nothing for her to do but wait. *Where is he*, she thought with annoyance. *Why hasn't Yassef shown him in yet?* She reviewed, for the tenth time, the list of items she planned to discuss with the doctor. She knew it by heart. She reached into her files for a medical journal she had been reading and opened it, shuffling blankly through the pages. She wanted to appear as if she were doing something.

"Excuse me." A deep voice at the door interrupted her thoughts.

Shannon looked up and her heart jumped. Standing in the door was a tall, broad-shouldered man. His rugged, tanned features and his dark blond hair highlighted by the sun told her he was a man who enjoyed the great outdoors. His eyes were a strange shade of blue—lighter than any she had ever seen—and they seemed to look right through her.

Shannon hadn't imagined that her new employee would look like this at all. She had expected him to be lean and dark, perhaps; an intellectual, not this brawny, golden-haired man who looked like he would be more at home in a rough-knit sweater and boots than a doctor's smock and surgical gloves.

Nor had she expected to feel so nervous. She was at a loss for words. "Yes?" she finally ventured, feeling that simple word was almost more than she could handle.

"Pardon me. I'm looking for Dr. Mallison," he answered.

"I'm Dr. Mallison." Shannon smiled and extended her hand. "You must be Dr. Sinclair."

"I'm sorry!" he apologized. "I didn't know . . . ."

"That I was a woman? Perhaps I should have made it clear. My name does confuse people sometimes."

Shannon was doing everything she could to appear confident and in control. But her pulse was racing and she was trembling. In an effort to overcome the anxiety she was feeling she thumbed through the papers on her desk, hoping to appear efficient rather than flustered and confused. She found the little list of topics she wanted to discuss. With a sigh she placed it in easy view to one side of her desk.

With a start Shannon realized that Cliff Sinclair was standing before her silently, his hands on his hips, a gentle smile on his lips. Could he tell how nervous she was? His blue eyes seemed to be taking in every move she made. Shannon did everything she could to avoid looking at him.

"Oh! Please, sit down," she said abruptly, embarrassed to have kept him standing for so long. "You'll have to excuse me. I'm not usually this disorganized." Shannon played nervously with the journal she had been skimming when he came in.

"Thank you," he answered, lowering himself into a comfortable armchair. "But we'll have to argue over who is the disorganized one. It seems to me I'm the one at fault here, if you don't mind a contender for the honor."

His voice was relaxed, deep, low and melodic. Shannon loved the sound of it and found herself getting caught up in its gentle rhythm. With a start, she realized that he didn't have a French accent. Where was he from, she wondered.

"No, I won't quarrel with you." She smiled. He had an easy way about him that helped her feel relaxed. "Do you mind if I ask you a question?"

"Of course not!" he responded, smiling.

With a start Shannon realized how stupid her words were under the circumstances.

"I mean . . . a personal sort of question, not. . . ." Shannon stopped. How could she be making such a fool of herself?

She glanced nervously at him. His eyes met hers for what seemed an eternal, vibrant moment. Shannon finally looked away and again tried to get her bearings. What was it they had been talking about?

"You were going to ask . . . ."

"Yes! But it's nothing. I'm embarrassed to be making anything of it. I only wanted to know where you were from. I thought you were French, and yet, from your voice, you sound like you might be American."

"A Virginian. My father has a legal firm in Richmond. But my mother is French. Until I was fourteen, we lived in Paris. Then we moved to Richmond, my father's hometown. I moved back to Paris to go to university, and I've been living in France ever since . . . until now, that is. And you. . . are you American, too?"

"Yes. My father was a lawyer in San Francisco."

"Really. I wonder if they . . . ."

"I'm afraid not. You see, my father died many years ago."

"I'm sorry. . . ."

"Don't worry. It's been a long time."

Shannon paused, her big, gray eyes clouding over. It wasn't true. It didn't seem so long ago anymore. The death of her grandfather, a man she had loved very much, continued to haunt her. And the old grief over the death of her parents seemed greater now than it ever had before.

In spite of herself, tears came to her eyes. Quickly she turned her head and reached to pull a hand-kerchief from her purse. Where was it, she thought with mortification, the tears now out of control and streaming down her cheeks. "I'm so sorry," she whispered hoarsely, hiding her face in her hands. "It's just that . . . ." But her words were engulfed by a sob

Feeling more and more embarrassed, Shannon made an effort to get herself under control. She stood and stumbled for the door. "Please . . . excuse me for a moment," she muttered in a broken voice. But Cliff Sinclair's hand on her arm stopped her.

"You don't have to leave on my account," he said gently, his eyes telling her that everything was all right, that there was no need to run.

How could he understand? She had only met him, and yet she felt that she had known him for a long time. She stared at him, mesmerized.

"Will this help?" he asked, offering her a handkerchief.

Shannon nodded and wiped the tears from her cheeks. She still didn't trust her voice—she was afraid of breaking down again.

"I'm sorry. I'm never like this," she apologized. It was true. She had always been a very controlled, unemotional woman—the one person everyone could count on to keep a level head in a crisis. But since her grandfather had died, she was beginning to have emotional outbursts that were quite unlike her. There had been that episode with Carol a week ago; she and Carol were still not speaking because of it. And now—bursting into tears in front of the new surgeon, and a world-famous surgeon at that. She didn't know what to make of it.

"Dr. Charles Mallison was my grandfather. We were very close. I guess I'm still upset over his death."

Shannon walked back to her desk and sat down.

"There, I feel better now. Thank you for being so understanding." She sighed deeply and tried to relax, making sure she would not have another outburst.

"It's only natural. It happens to everyone at some time," Cliff Sinclair said, easing himself into the armchair once more. "It's happened to me, so I know how you feel."

Shannon glanced toward the surgeon. She wondered what he meant. She smiled and started to look away but his eyes held hers for a long, meaningful moment.

"Well," Shannon said with a laugh. "This is quite an introduction. I hope you're not having second thoughts about coming to join us."

Cliff Sinclair smiled broadly and chuckled. With a good-natured shrug he shook his head. "In fact, I'm liking it more and more," he said.

"Did you have a good trip? The heat isn't too much for you, I hope."

"Not at all. I stopped over in Cairo for a few days to visit a friend, so I've had some time to get used to it."

"I had intended that we take this opportunity to get to know one another better. We didn't have much of a chance to do that in our brief correspondence," Shannon said. She was feeling completely at ease now, and relaxed. "I had also made a list of things to go over with you, but under the circumstances, I think they can wait until later."

"Excuse me, but before we can go on," he said, "I just want to tell you I didn't come to Aswan alone. I brought someone with me. I'm sorry, but I just didn't have time to inform you of my plans before I arrived."

"Your wife?" Shannon asked quickly, watching him closely.

"No, a friend. Oh, don't worry, everything is okay," he added. "It's just that circumstances forced me to bring her along. I promised a good friend of mine I would look out for her and see that she was all right. I couldn't very well do that if I left her in France, could I? So I brought her along. She finds herself in rather difficult circumstances at the moment and . . . I'm sorry I didn't let you know she was coming," he said abruptly. "But I just didn't have time to write and tell you."

He had explained the situation in a calm manner. Shannon couldn't tell what he really felt about it.

"Are you counting on having your friend stay here on the hospital grounds?" Shannon asked.

"I would be very grateful if . . . ."

"The trouble is, I'm afraid it's not possible. We only have room for our staff."

"I understand perfectly, but you see, Divina Bayeul is an anesthetist and has excellent references. I thought you might have a place for her. I was really hoping we could come to some kind of agreement."

"I would be delighted to hire her, but I'm afraid I

can't. Our financial situation is rather tight at the moment . . . . Besides, now that you're here to head our surgical team, we have everyone we need. I'm sure you'll find your colleagues here fully competent and qualified to assist you in every area of your work."

"I'm sure they are," he replied. "However, I prefer to work with Divina. She's been my anesthetist for a year now and we're used to working with each other. You might say we're a team." He looked at Shannon, noting her dubious expression, then continued quietly.

"Please understand me. I'm really not trying to be bullheaded, although I know it must seem that way to you. It's just that I have a moral obligation to look after this woman. I couldn't, in good conscience, send her off on her own. I want to work here; I'm sure it could work out quite well for all of us. But you see, I have no choice."

Shannon didn't like being put in this position. She needed him but he wouldn't stay unless this woman worked with him. What could she do? There was a backlog of patients scheduled for surgery and she just didn't have the time to look around for another doctor. She would have to start all over from the beginning—correspondence, checking references—it could be months before she filled the position. She didn't have that kind of time to waste. The situation was urgent and called for extraordinary measures.

"Well, it looks like you've got me over a barrel," she said quietly. "I need a surgeon right away and you won't stay unless your friend works with you here at the Foundation. But I'm afraid I couldn't let you both live in the house reserved for the resident surgeon. Because of our space shortage, you have to share the house with two other members of our staff."

"I'm afraid you don't understand. Divina and I are just friends—nothing more. We're not romantically involved. I have a moral obligation to look after her. She's an excellent anesthetist, but that's beside the point. She has to stay with me, at least for the time being. But I feel badly about putting you in this position. Listen to this—what if she worked for free? I think she might agree to that, under the circumstances. That way, you keep to your budget and I can live with my conscience."

Shannon was stunned. His suggestion seemed like a sound one—temporarily, at least. *What do I have to lose*, she thought. *If the woman is easy to get along with and a good worker, everything could work out perfectly.* She could transfer Marika Stenberg to obstetrics. They need the extra help. Having weighed the pros and cons of the situation, Shannon decided to hire the woman, subject, of course, to an interview with her.

What kind of salary would Miss Bayeul eventually expect?"

"I think she would be open to any reasonable offer."

"What do you mean by reasonable?"

"Well, that's up to you."

"All right," Shannon sighed. "But, I want you to know that I'm still upset by your methods."

"I don't like them anymore than you do, believe me. It's just that, given the circumstances, I can't do anything else," he reassured her gravely.

Shannon said nothing and stood up to indicate that the conversation was over. She walked slowly across the room and opened the door.

In the outer office, Divina Bayeul was standing quietly by the bay window looking out at the garden. She was tall and slim and her dark hair was shown off to great advantage by her light green linen suit. When she heard the door open, she turned slowly and looked at Shannon. She was young, and gave the impression of being barely out of her teens. Her face was narrow, her complexion smooth, her eyes dark and mysterious.

"Would you come in please, Miss Bayeul?" Shannon asked politely.

A few minutes later, she had Divina's references on the desk in front of her. According to her papers, she was twenty-six years old and had spent some time working at the Iris clinic.

"Don't you have a passport?" Shannon asked curiously.

"Yes, I do. I put it in the outer pocket of my flight bag just after I went through customs at the airport," Divina replied quickly. "My bags are still out in the hall. If you would like to see it, I can just . . . ."

Shannon cut her short. "If I understand Dr. Sinclair correctly, you left France in a hurry. How did you manage to get a visa on such short notice?"

"Cliff has a friend in Cairo who cut through a lot of red tape for us at the consulate."

In a few moments, everything was settled. Shannon had explained the financial situation and while Divina clearly wasn't happy about working on a volunteer basis, she conceded that it was better than nothing at all. And in time, no doubt, she would move into a paid position.

"There's a vacant room in the house where the head nurses live," Shannon suggested. "You could stay there, if you like."

"That would be fine. Thank you," Divina replied, a sad note in her voice.

Shannon didn't want to prolong the interview. The main points had been discussed and Divina seemed anxious to leave. In the course of their rather brief interview, the woman had been very quiet and had scarcely said a word. She had been distant, mournful and aloof.

Shannon rang for Yassef and got to her feet. "Yassef will carry your bags and show you to your quarters," she said gently. In spite of the mystery and sadness that seemed to hand around Divina, Shannon liked her. "If you wish, we can meet again later at dinner and I can introduce you to the rest of the staff. There's a communal dining room on the compound. I think you'll like it."

Shannon stood at the window and watched her two new employees follow Yassef across the garden. Cliff Sinclair walked with an easy, loping motion.

Beside him the anesthetist seemed tiny and frail. He stopped to help her down some steep stone steps, taking her gently by the elbow. As he did so, Shannon saw him look back toward the hospital, scanning the building before he turned. Then they went their separate ways, exchanging a fleeting glance, but saying nothing.

Chapter 5

A few hours later, there was a luncheon for the two new staff members, who were presented to their co-workers. Much to Shannon's delight, the staff greeted their new colleagues with warmth and respect. This would augur well for the future of the hospital, she thought happily. Earlier that morning, after the interviews, she had seen Jason and told him how Cliff had insisted that she find a place for Divina on the staff. Jason hadn't thought much of it, and Shannon found herself making excuses for the new surgeon.

"I think he was sincere when he said circumstances forced him to act this way. He said he was sorry, and I believe him. Maybe someday, we'll find out why he had to bring her here with him."

In spite of herself, Shannon was intrigued by this unexpected turn of events. What did Divina really mean to him, she wondered curiously. Was she just a friend as he had said? She found that hard to believe, especially when the relationship in question was between two such incredibly attractive people, who obviously seemed bound together by some mysterious tie.

A couple of times during the meal, she caught him looking toward Divina very tenderly. The new anesthetist wore the same strange funny look of anger and sadness that she had presented that morning. She seemed shrouded in some kind of sorrow and, at times, looked completely lost and bewildered. Cliff had mentioned that she was in some kind of trouble, Shannon remembered. What could it be? Was she in some kind of trouble with the law? What was she running from? What was she trying to hide? What secret lay behind those dark, enigmatic eyes?

Shannon bridled her imagination and scolded herself for such fruitless speculation. After all, she reminded herself, their private life was none of her business. The only things she need be concerned about were their professional abilities and the manner in which they conducted themselves at the hospital. If they proved to be serious, competent professionals, she couldn't be more satisfied.

"When do you plan to start working, Cliff?" she asked, as the meal drew to a close.

"As soon as possible," he replied.

"Before you do, I'd like to show you around the hospital. Perhaps this afternoon," she suggested.

"First, I'd like to see the case histories of those patients needing emergency surgery."

"Of course. Meet me at my office at five-thirty. Later, I can give you and Divina the grand tour."

SHANNON WAS JUST changing into a fresh white coat when Cliff arrived in her office.

"I just got here myself," she said, as he walked in the door. "I was held up in maternity. A difficult delivery—the woman gave birth to twins. They were so small and weak we had to put them in incubators immediately. Dr. Hinawi was prepared for this, though, because the mother was severely under-nourished and weakened by the rigors of the preg-nancy. So many pregnant woman are in that state in this part of the country. Unfortunately . . . ." Her words trailed off as it occurred to her yet again that there was no easy solution to this problem.

Cliff looked at her pensively, a serious expression on his handsome face, but said nothing.

"Sit down, won't you? And I'll tell you about your patients," she continued briskly, determined to be entirely professional in this encounter with the handsome surgeon.

As she took a pile of file folders out of the cabinet standing by the wall of her office, Cliff watched her closely. Realizing she was the focus of his attention, Shannon began talking rapidly. "Before going through these case histories, I would like to tell you about the Mallison Foundation. I think it would be helpful if you knew something about the background of the place where you're going to be working."

He nodded silently and, when she realized he was sitting there waiting for her to continue, she took a deep breath and began. She outlined the beginnings of the hospital that had meant so much to her grandfather. Charles, she explained, had died just when his work was starting to bear fruit. Briefly, she described to him how Dr. Mallison had run the hospital for so many years.

"When he died," she continued; "I decided to take over the administration of the hospital and find another surgeon as soon as possible. I hope you'll be happy here, doctor, and I also think the good feelings among the other members of the staff will facilitate your work here. We're a closely knit little group and every one of us is devoted to the Foundation. Each staff member considers his work here his own personal project—and they're right. After all, if it weren't for them and their dedication, we would cease to exist."

"Is this the only hospital in Aswan?" Cliff asked.

"No, there's a public hospital, too. Three hundred beds. It was built around the same time as the High Dam. But ours serves a very definite need in the community. You see, although the Aswan High Dam has turned the desert into a life-giving, fertile land, it has also brought disease—and one disease in particular: schistosomiasis, or bilharzia.

"This disease, which my grandfather spent his life studying, is spread by the snails that live in the irrigation canals. Tiny worms get into the intestines and bladder. They don't kill their host, but they weaken the vital organs and shorten the victim's life. Since the building of the dam, this disease has been on the increase. According to official figures, sixty percent of the population now carries the virus. And this is the disease my grandfather was committed to fighting. That's why he built the hospital.

"He loved this country. He was stationed here when he was a young doctor in the army. Then, after his discharge, he came into a large fortune. My grandmother was dead by then, and his children were all grown up, so he decided to build the Foundation. Later, he added a maternity ward and a child welfare section to combat the high rate of infant mortality. It all went very well for a while. However, over the years, the resources and personnel required to provide those services have increased. Today we have barely enough staff to handle our demands, and we're fast running out of money. Nevertheless, I want you to realize that, as far as it's possible, your job here is secure."

"I suppose you can't expand right now," Cliff said quietly, thinking of research programs.

"Well, as I already told you, we just don't have the money to do that. Not now. Our income is very small, and so far we haven't received the subsidy we need so badly from the Egyptian government. My grandfather wasn't a businessman. He had no idea what could happen once the hospital really got going. He thought he could limit the services offered here, but he soon found out that was impossible. You can't turn away sick people just because they can't pay. He poured everything he had into this hospital—but it still wasn't enough.

"So I'm facing some pretty difficult problems right now. However, I'm sure everything is going to work out," she said quickly, not wanting to leave him with an unfavorable impression of the Foundation. "We'll make out all right. I'm determined to persuade the Egyptian government to give us the money we need."

On that note, she turned to the file folder in front of her and handed it to Cliff. "If you want to study this emergency case, you'll find all the necessary information here: X rays, the medical history and Jason's report."

WHEN DIVINA JOINED SHANNON and Cliff at six o'clock she found them deeply engrossed in setting up the surgery timetable.

"Cliff and I are just finishing up now, Divina," Shannon announced as she looked up into the woman's smooth, masklike face. "If you wait just a moment, we can begin our tour of the hospital."

The first stop on the tour included the offices, the kitchen and the laundry facilities. The two newcomers were quick to notice that everything was clean and extremely well organized.

When Shannon opened the door to the outer office of the pharmacy, she found two nurse's aides preparing a tray of bandages and antiseptics. After introducing them to her new staff members, she took out her key to the dispensary, pushed open the door and led Cliff and Divina inside.

"Of course, our stock isn't complete by any means," she explained, pointing to the bottles of medicine neatly labelled and sorted on the shelves, "but we do have a variety of medication here that meets our needs."

"How do you get your medicines?" Divina asked, speaking for the first time. Cliff Sinclair turned his head sharply and stared at Shannon.

"Well, as you know, drugs are pretty scarce in Egypt. So we get most of what we need from Europe, the Red Cross, agencies set up to help under-developed countries and some private donations. However, no matter how helpful and generous people are, we always end up spending a great deal of money on drugs."

"Do you have enough money coming in to cover most of your expenses?" Cliff asked, changing the subject.

"I'm afraid not. Without the private donations from certain wealthy people in Aswan, we wouldn't survive." Cliff nodded. Divina looked down and slowly walked out of the dispensary, followed by Cliff and Shannon. As she stepped out into the hall, she almost bumped into Carol, who was standing there in her bathing suit.

"What on earth are you doing here dressed like that?" Shannon asked in amazement.

"I was swimming in the river," Carol replied, tossing her curly red hair back off her face and staring deliberately at her stepsister. "I stepped on a piece of glass and now I've got a big gash in my heel. It's not deep but I wanted to put some disinfectant on it right away. I couldn't find any back at the house so I came here."

"Go see Ann Clark in room A," Shannon said quietly, looking down at the blood-stained bandage on Carol's foot. "She can clean the wound for you and bandage it up properly."

Carol gave Divina a quick nod and let her provocative eyes linger on Cliff, but then she obediently hobbled down the hall in search of Ann Clark.

For an instant, Shannon's emotions were in total confusion under the strain Carol's presence aroused in her these days. But then she gave herself a small shake and snapped her attention back to the present. Cliff and Divina hadn't seemed to notice anything unusual in the incident, or if they had, they weren't saying anything.

The tour continued without further mishap. They moved on to the offices of the head nurses and went through all the various departments. Finally, Shannon opened the door to the room that would be Cliff's office. It was airy and bright, it overlooked the garden and it was situated next to the operating room.

With an appreciative glance, Cliff wordlessly took in every aspect of the office and silently conveyed his approval. "I think I'll do very good work here," he commented finally.

Shannon, to her surprise, found she had been anxiously waiting for his opinion. She gave a small sigh of relief and smiled.

The tour ended, Shannon left them to settle into the office, not realizing that before long, the presence of Divina and Cliff would bring the quiet, peaceful days at Mallison Hospital to an end.

THAT EVENING, around nine o'clock, Jason decided to visit Shannon in her office. She could be found there most evenings, going over the accounts for the day. It was one of the few times during their busy schedule when they could see each other in relative peace, long after everyone else had left for the day. When he saw the light on in her window, he hurried to catch her before she went home.

"What do you think of our new colleagues?" she asked, as soon as he came in.

"Quite nice, but the young woman is very reserved and withdrawn," he replied.

"What do you mean?" Shannon asked curiously.

"Well, there's something about her that's kind of secretive and reticent. I don't know what it is, exactly. Whenever you mention the past, she becomes vague, evasive, almost as if she had something to hide. She always seems to be on guard."

"I know what you mean," Shannon agreed. "I noticed the same thing myself."

"Sinclair seems to be very open and expansive on every subject but one," Jason continued. "But Divina . . . ."

"Are you on a first name basis with her already?" Shannon interjected.

"Her name suits her, doesn't it? A beautiful name for a beautiful woman. She's unusually lovely, or haven't you noticed?" he asked slyly.

"Of course I have," she said calmly, not rising to the bait. "What were you going to say about her?"

"She's almost like a recluse. Enigmatic, mysterious. A real loner. You'd have a good deal of trouble discovering what she's thinking."

"Do you think there's anything between them?" Shannon asked after a short pause.

"Who knows?" Jason said, shrugging his shoulders. "Time will tell, I guess. But right now, how about leaving those dull old accounts and taking a walk in the garden with me? Or don't you think that would be proper?" he teased, noting her hesitation.

"Oh, no, it's not that. It's just that I haven't finished here yet."

"You've worked long enough for one day, Shannon," he said, taking her by the shoulders and forcing her gently to her feet. "Come on. A nice walk is just what you need. In fact, it will do us both good."

Realizing he wasn't going to take no for an answer, Shannon turned the lights out in her office. In the sudden darkness, Jason pulled her into his arms and kissed her deeply. Feeling his strong arms around her, she tried to relax and give herself over to his warm embrace. When they drew apart, she smiled gently and let him lead her down the long, dimly lit halls of the hospital, empty now except for the occasional night nurse.

When they stepped outside, they were greeted by a brilliant full moon and a cool, fresh breeze, fragrant with the scent of flowers. As they strolled through the gardens, the light wind from the river gently caressed their faces, bringing with it the heady fragrance of the beautiful jasmine. It was a lovely evening, and they walked slowly in the shadow of the hospital wall.

Suddenly, Shannon stopped and clutched Jason's arm. "Look," she whispered.

Outlined sharply in the pale moonlight was a shadowy silhouette, flitting quickly across the lawn in the direction of Cliff's house. It was Divina. When she reached the front porch, she slipped inside the house and noiselessly closed the door behind her.

Suddenly, Cliff's words came back to her: "Divina and I are just good friends. Nothing more." *I wonder*, Shannon thought, smiling faintly.

Chapter 6

In the days that followed, Shannon was not aware of any more clandestine meetings between Cliff and Divina, and she had seen nothing to indicate that there might be a secret relationship between them. There were no knowing glances or meaningful smiles, at least as far as she could tell.

Except for dinner, which took place in a relaxed, informal atmosphere with six people at a table, Cliff and Divina were never seen together. They saw each other only during working hours. If they did sit together at dinner, they indulged in only the most banal and superficial conversation, or talked purely shop. Divina didn't seem to be seeking out Cliff's company, and often ended up sitting quietly with Carol at another table.

Before long, Shannon realized that Cliff was, indeed, a brilliant surgeon, worthy of his reputation.

She was honored to have the opportunity to work with someone of his stature. It awed her to watch him work and the number of things she was learning from him excited her tremendously. He was quick and decisive, and he had that clean, crisp technique found in surgeons from the Paris school. There was no doubt about it—he was a master in his field.

Divina, on the other hand, was a good anesthetist, but there was nothing extraordinary about her work.

Why had a man like Sinclair, who obviously had a great talent and a brilliant future, left a promising career in Paris to work in an obscure little clinic in Aswan? Shannon couldn't help puzzling over the question. And why had Divina come with him if, as he said, there was nothing between them?

She found herself asking the same questions over and over again and, before long, she decided that there was definitely something very strange going on.

During their first days in Aswan, the two newcomers suffered terribly from the heat that was becoming more and more unbearable every day. Once their work was over, they would go straight back to their respective houses and disappear. Divina never went into town in the evenings, and seemed content to take short walks in the garden.

When the heat of the day finally gave way to the cooler air of the evening, Cliff would often sit out on the porch of his house, reading or playing checkers with Bechir Hinawi, Jason or one of the two men with whom he shared the house.

Almost before she realized it, Shannon found

herself more and more drawn to Cliff. The attraction was subtle, and she wasn't really aware of her feelings toward him. She was completely absorbed in her work at the hospital and still spent all her free time with Jason. But, as the days passed, she was becoming fascinated by the new surgeon on staff. He was quiet yet manly. He never talked about himself and, aside from knowing him in a professional capacity, she knew nothing about him at all. He was a mystery, and there was every indication he was going to maintain his intriguing privacy. Shannon sometimes wished she could break down his reserve, but she couldn't. He was always silent on the subject of his past, and Divina was equally reticent.

Then, one day, Cliff told Shannon he had to go to the consulate at six o'clock that evening to clear up some matters concerning his work permit and his employment as head surgeon at the Mallison Foundation. Shannon had forgotten all about this and, when she left the hospital in her jeep, she was surprised to see Cliff heading toward the taxis that stood at the gates of the hospital property, waiting for prospective customers. When she remembered her conversation with him, she had Yassef stop the car immediately. "Can I drop you off in town, Cliff? I'm going right by the consulate."

Cliff gladly accepted her offer. As Yassef drove slowly down the road, he said, "Thanks for the lift, I was in no mood to haggle over cab fares."

"The next time you want to go into town, ask Yassef to do that for you. He knows the language, and all the tricks of the trade as well," she suggested kindly.

In spite of the blazing heat, the streets of Aswan were crowded with people out for a stroll or enjoying an evening coffee at one of the many sidewalk cafes. The traffic wasn't heavy, however, and Yassef easily maneuvered the jeep through the narrow, winding streets that led to the center of the newer section of the city.

As they drove along, Shannon glanced at Cliff as unobtrusively as possible. His eyes seemed to wander aimlessly over the people and the sights around him, his handsome face lost in a kind of melancholy reverie.

"I'm going to visit a young woman who is expecting her first baby," Shannon announced, trying to begin a conversation that would establish some contact with him. "She lives quite near the consulate, so I can drop you off at the door, if you like."

"You mean that after a busy day like yours, you still have time to make house calls?" he said with surprise.

"Sometimes I do. This girl is the second oldest daughter of a very important man in Aswan. He wants his daughter to have the baby at home, like all the other women in his family, but he wants someone there to see that everything goes all right. A few years ago there was an accident, and ever since then, he's wanted people from the Foundation there to help."

"What kind of accident?"

"Ben Aroual's wife died in childbirth. He thought

the midwife who was assisting at the birth didn't know what she was doing and called my grandfather for help. Unfortunately, he didn't call the Foundation in time. The child survived, but the mother died. From that day on, Ben Aroual called my grandfather in every time one of the women in his household was about to give birth. Now that grandfather has died, I've taken his place." She paused, looking at the passing scenery and thinking about the man whose daughter she would be visiting.

"Ben Aroual is one of the most important men in the city. We're on very good terms and he gives the Foundation annual donations. He's a banker, and very close to the Governor. He's given us a great deal of financial and moral support over the years. It seems to me this is the least I can do in return for all his help."

Cliff smiled at her and she could tell his eyes were appraising her. Then, suddenly, a turn in the road threw them off balance. Cliff flung his arm across Shannon to brace himself, and to keep from crushing her. His awkward position put his face within inches of hers. As his proud blue eyes stared into hers, Shannon's heart began to pound disconcertingly. For a moment, she had the silly notion that Cliff Sinclair was about to kiss her. But as she lowered her lashes in consternation, he pulled away from her and regained his seat as the car straightened out. Shannon could still feel the pressure of his broad, muscular chest against her in her imagination, and she gave a little involuntary shiver.

"Oh, there's something I've been wanting to ask,"

Cliff said, breaking the pregnant silence. "Are you satisfied with the work we're doing?"

"I am . . . very much," Shannon replied haltingly, finding it difficult to switch back to the professional mode after such close physical contact.

"Are you sorry about Divina?" he inquired.

Even if she did have questions about Divina, Shannon knew she couldn't have said so. After all, Cliff had made it quite clear that he wouldn't work at the Foundation unless Divina was there, too. But Shannon felt no pressure to lie to him about Divina. She was one of the vital links in the chain of personnel at the hospital now, and was doing an acceptable job. In answer to his question, Shannon conceded that she was satisfied with Divina's work. In fact, Divina was fast becoming indispensable to the clinic.

"I'm glad," Cliff said, with a sigh of relief. "I have to admit that I've been feeling guilty about the whole thing," he added, turning to look out the window as if nothing had happened.

The jeep was rolling along a wide avenue that followed the banks of the Nile. Even at this time of the day, the sun was dazzling. Down by the river banks, impervious to the burning heat, children of all ages were playing ball in the sparse grass by the water. Not far from them, heavily veiled women were sitting on the ground watching over their children, while the men huddled together in the shade of a big tree, engaged in a lively conversation.

In the distance, Shannon noticed a crusie ship, the *Osiris*, just pulling into the wharf, its decks heavy with crowds of expectant tourists.

Cliff gazed at the river· and the activity on its banks. "Have you lived in Aswan a long time?" he asked suddenly.

"Almost eleven years," she answered with a start. His words had distracted her from her contemplation of the life pulsating around them.

Cliff unbuttoned his collar and pulled it away from his burning skin. "Do you ever get used to the heat?" he asked with a laugh.

"That depends on when you get here," she explained. "I arrived in September, so I had time to get used to some warm weather before the real heat began. You didn't have the chance to get used to it gradually, like I did. I hope you can; this hot, dry climate is really good for you. We've got most of July and August to go," she continued, "and they're going to be killers. Sometimes the temperature rises as high as a hundred and twenty during the day. But there's one good thing—the early evenings are beautiful and, when it gets dark, the nights are often cool."

"Does it ever rain?"

"Hardly ever. I can count on one hand the number of times it's rained since I've been here."

"Now I understand why so many of the houses don't have roofs!" he said wryly.

"Did you know much about Egypt before you came to Aswan?"

"About four years ago I visited a friend of mine in Cairo, but I really didn't get to know the country. I didn't stay long enough."

By this time, the car had turned off the wide avenue and was rolling quietly along a shady little street. Shannon asked Yassef to stop at the next intersection, and then she turned to Cliff. "See that white building over there by that clump of palm trees? That's the American consulate."

The American flag hung proudly over the door of the consulate, which was surrounded by a flower garden. As Yassef parked the car, Cliff buttoned up his shirt collar and put on his jacket. Then, as he stepped out onto the sidewalk, he turned and looked at Shannon. "Thanks for the ride," he said graciously, bending through the car's open window. His handsome, rugged face showed genuine gratitude.

Shannon turned away. She found Cliff's manner disquieting. His blue eyes were so piercing, so unsettling.

"Are you going to be long?" Shannon asked impulsively.

"No, I'll only be a few minutes. I just have to sign a couple of documents and then I'll be finished."

"Well, then, why don't I wait for you here?" she suggested. "I'd like you to come along with me to Ben Aroual's place and meet him. I think you'll like him—he's a very intelligent, cultured man. And I know he'd be honored to meet you."

"I'd love to meet him," Cliff said, smiling engagingly.

With a slight feeling of misgiving, Shannon watched Cliff disappear inside the consulate. Should she have invited him along, she wondered. Wouldn't this unexpected visit inconvenience Ben Aroual? After all, it wasn't a terrific idea to arrive at anyone's house with an extra guest. And what would Jason think of her impulsive invitation? *What's the matter with me*, she scolded herself impatiently. *I don't have to justify my actions to Jason—or anyone else.* But no matter how hard she tried, she couldn't shake the uneasy feeling that settled in the pit of her stomach as she waited for Cliff to return.

He wasn't long. He jumped back into the car and Yassef pulled away from the curb and drove slowly down the street. The sun was lower in the sky now and the heat was beginning to abate slightly, as it did each day at dusk.

Before long, Yassef drove through the gates of a vast estate and up the long, narrow driveway that led to Ben Aroual's sumptuous home. In front of the house was a large white plaster basin, where lotus flowers lazily floated in cool green water. The house itself was elegant in its antiquity and simple classic lines.

A maid opened the door and led Shannon and Cliff across a large foyer tiled with highly polished stones to a room furnished in oriental fashion with low, soft couches, inlaid tables and expensive bric-a-brac.

"Well, this is certainly a far cry from the little village near the Foundation," Cliff remarked.

"Don't judge Ben Aroual by the comfort of his home or the thickness of his rugs," Shannon warned him. "He's a very conscientious man who is deeply concerned and involved with the problems of his fellow man. With the help of a few energetic men like himself, he's doing all he can to better conditions for the sick and the poor in this city. His task is an enormous one, though. And no matter how much he does, it just seems like a drop in the bucket."

Shannon stopped talking abruptly as the door opened and Ben Aroual walked into the room. It was difficult to tell how old he was but his eyes, which shone brilliantly in his face, were lively and intelligent. He was wearing the traditional long cotton robe and white leather sandals.

Shannon proceeded to make the introductions. "I thought you would like to meet our new surgeon, Dr. Cliff Sinclair. You've always been so interested in everything that goes on at the hospital."

"Dr. Cliff Sinclair . . . the French surgeon? I'm honored. Still . . . stepping into Charles's shoes is a pretty big job," he said, smiling over at Cliff. "But I'm sure you're more than up to it."

At that moment, a servant appeared carrying a tray of turkish coffee and small cakes.

"I had one of the servants tell Fawzia you're here," Ben Aroual commented as he proceeded to serve the coffee and cake to his guests. "Someone will come for you when she's ready to see you."

They didn't have to wait long. When Shannon followed the servant out of the room, Aroual turned and looked at Cliff, his dark eyes shining. "You seem to think quite a lot of Shannon, doctor," he noted bluntly.

Taken off guard by his abrupt and rather surprising question, Cliff had to think for a minute before answering. He admitted to himself that he had been having difficulty taking his eyes off her.

"Well, to tell you truth, the only contact we have is at work. So I haven't really had a chance to get to know her yet. But, so far, I'm quite impressed by her—she's a very fine woman."

"She is," the older man replied fondly. "I admire her intelligence, courage and spunk. She's got a good head on her shoulders. I know there must be times when she gets very discouraged, but she never admits defeat. Shannon was never groomed or adequately prepared for the work she's doing now. Being the administrator of a hospital that's in financial difficulty requires a certain toughness of mind and a very strong will. One must have the courage of one's convictions in a position like that. I'm happy to see Dr. Wilfred is helping her all he can."

"I didn't realize he was," Cliff said, surprised.

"Well, if the talk about them is true," the older man continued, smiling brightly, "they'll be married soon. That will be wonderful for Shannon." He looked at his guest. "You seem surprised. Didn't you know they were engaged?"

"Nothing's been said about it in my hearing."

"Would you like more coffee?" Aroual asked politely, changing the subject to cover any possible embarrassment on the doctor's part.

"Yes, please."

"Would it be prying if I asked you what made you give up your work in Paris to come to work in Aswan?" Aroual asked as he tended to his guest's request.

"Not at all. I left because I wanted a change of scene. I wanted to try something different," Cliff replied. Much to his relief, he heard Shannon's footsteps in the hall and sighed imperceptibly as Ben

Aroual got to his feet and inquired after his daughter's condition.

"Fawzia is doing very nicely. It's a normal pregnancy, and there's nothing to worry about at all," Shannon announced happily.

"Are you sure she'll be all right? I mean, there's no chance of anything going wrong, is there?" Aroual asked anxiously. "She's never been strong and I'm just worried that . . . ."

"You don't have a thing to worry about," Shannon interrupted gently. "In three months, you'll be the proud grandfather of a beautiful, healthy baby."

"I hope it's a boy!" the older man exclaimed.

"Your son-in-law says he doesn't care what sex the baby is," Shannon commented, a teasing light in her eyes.

"I know. But still," he said, "I want a grandson."

"HOW DID YOU LIKE BEN AROUAL?" Shannon asked Cliff on the way back to the hospital.

"I enjoyed talking with him. He's a cultivated man, honest and open, and he speaks beautiful English. No trace of an accent at all. I would like to see him again."

"Don't worry, you will. He comes by the hospital every now and then to see how we're doing."

The sun had set and night had fallen suddenly upon the city. From the towering height of a nearby minaret came the nasal chanting of the muezzin calling people to prayer. Shannon and Cliff lapsed into an emotionally-charged silence.

Yassef stopped the car in front of a small bakery to pick up the pastries Shannon had ordered earlier that day. On the brightly-lit street corners, merchants carrying trays of cakes and sweet buns were hawking their wares.

Yassef's sudden departure made Shannon uncomfortable. It was dark in the car, and the noise and gaiety outside made her feel as if she and Cliff were in their own very private world. She became aware of her every movement. Was he watching her? She stared fixedly out the window. Then, timidly, she glanced toward him, and her heart jumped. He was looking straight at her.

"Ben Aroual asked me what I thought of you," he finally said, breaking the silence between them.

"Of me? What a strange question for him to ask." Shannon tried to laugh and nervously threw her head back against the seat.

A heavy silence fell between them again. Shannon's pulse raced. Frantically, she wondered if he could hear it.

"Aren't you going to ask what I said?" Cliff whispered with a teasing grin, leaning toward her.

"No," Shannon said, teasing him in return, trying hard to keep a straight face.

"I said I didn't know you very well . . . yet."

Shannon was afraid to speak. She wondered what he meant—and she also wondered how to answer him. But Cliff broke the silence.

"Ben Aroual also said that you and Jason Wilfred were engaged to be married."

"But how would he know something like that?" She gasped.

"Then it's true?"

"I can't say," Shannon said simply, staring blankly

in front of her. With relief, she caught sight of Yassef leaving the shop and heading for the car.

SHANNON AND CLIFF were working later that week in her office on the diagnoses of some problem cases when Jason knocked and entered.

"Shannon, there's something I must talk to you about," Jason said abruptly, not even acknowledging Cliff's presence.

"What is it?" she replied distractedly, still immersed in the file before her.

"Privately," he demanded.

"Is it business?" Jason nodded. "You can speak in front of Cliff. There are no secrets—from anyone."

"I insist," he said gruffly.

"Okay," Shannon said with a sigh of exasperation. She and Cliff had been intending to complete these files all week, and they had been making excellent progress this afternoon. "Let's go to the conference room."

Cliff had already made motions to leave, but Shannon asked him to stay. "I'll be right back. I'm eager to get this work done."

Jason led the way into the small conference room. The space was entirely taken up by one large table and numerous chairs. He sat in the first seat he could reach, motioning Shannon to one close to him.

"What's this all about?" Shannon asked, growing alarmed at Jason's manner. He looked quite upset.

"We've got trouble. It looks like someone's been filching amyl nitrate from the dispensary in large quantities."

"What!"

"Yes." Jason nodded gravely. Amyl nitrate was a drug administered to heart-attack patients. It was currently very popular in North American cities among the disco crowd—or so Jason had read in one of the weekly news magazines.

"But we don't carry large quantities of amyl nitrate. How could . . . ."

"That's just it, Shannon. Someone's been putting orders through in your name." Jason pulled a stack of green slips of paper from his pocket. "Here. Look at these."

Shannon looked through the stack. There were quite a few made out in her name . . . but not in her handwriting. And, the signatures were not always in the same hand. Some were round and open; some fluid with fancy scripts; still others were in a hand that nearly resembled printing. All of them looked like the handwriting of adolescents.

"Let's go talk to them," Shannon said, standing up "You can fill me in on the details on the way down."

The drug supply room was run by Beth and a new assistant. It didn't take long to find out that every single one of the orders had been put through at a time when the assistant was on duty alone, during lunches or breaks. The deliveries were made to a post-office box downtown.

"Didn't you find that strange?" Shannon asked the girl, who was terrified. The girl shook her head.

Shannon realized that the new assistant was simply not very bright. Her temper flaring, Shannon almost fired her, on the spot. She held her tongue, counted to ten and conceded that the girl could not be held responsible. She made a mental note to have the girl moved to a position that required a good public manner, which she had, but required no thought.

Shannon took a deep breath and looked around the dispensary. The situation was serious. If the story were to leak out to the general public, it could seriously hurt the Foundation's chance for government aid. Every hospital had to prove it had instituted—and maintained—the strictest control over its drugs. Shannon and Cliff got to work immediately, and in the next few days they set up a new release system that would be impossible to sabotage. Then they sent the writing samples on the green slips to experts in New York for analysis; each signature had been written by a different person. They were completely baffled.

Shannon finally brought the matter up with Jason, who confessed he had heard about it already through the hospital grapevine. The news was out.

Shannon immediately suspected Carol. She was compelled, under the circumstances, to search for evidence as much as she could, but she dreaded the possibility that some finger might actually point to her stepsister. Trafficking in serious drugs—and especially such a substantial amount of the drug— held a life sentence in Egypt. What would she do if the evidence pointed to Carol?

Shannon watched her stepsister for signs of strange behavior, but she saw none. Carol was normally erratic, and she was being every bit erratic as she had ever been before. She and Divina had apparently stopped sharing meals together, but that was the only noticeable difference in Carol's life. Over lunch, watching Carol at one end of the room and Divina at the other, Shannon noticed that Cliff was following her eyes exactly. She had told him her suspicions shortly after she had discussed the matter with Jason. He had looked stricken with the news, but had said nothing.

With time, the matter slipped into obscurity for want of any tangible evidence. Life appeared to be normal, and no more strange and inexplicable things happened—for the time being.

Chapter 7

The anniversary of the founding of the hospital was coming up and Shannon was planning a small party to celebrate the occasion. Since her grandfather's death, she hadn't met with the staff in a group as often as she'd originally planned; there just hadn't been time. But the idea was always on her mind, and she decided this happy occasion would be in perfect time to get them all together for an evening of enjoyment and relaxation.

There weren't many distractions for these men and women who worked long, hard hours inside the hospital walls. Granted, every now and then one of them took a short holiday or allowed himself a day off to do some sight-seeing among the ruins of ancient Egypt. There was so much to see: the vast stone quarries where the granite had been mined for the tombs of the Pharaohs so many centuries ago, the temple of Isis on the Island of Philo and the temple of Kom Ombo, whose walls were covered with bas relief and magnificent paintings. And in Aswan itself there was the Dam, of course, and Elephant Island, the palace of the Aga Khan and the botanical gardens. But, Shannon remained convinced the staff needed some time to enjoy themselves and put aside the misery and suffering they encountered in their work every day. In a relaxed, social atmosphere they could forget about business for a while.

When she told Jason her idea he agreed wholeheartedly.

"I think I'll have the party next week at my house," she announced. "I'll invite some people from the families we know in Aswan and the entire medical staff. It won't be just us—that's the last thing we need. We see each other day in and day out. Having people from town will be like a breath of fresh air and it'll expand everyone's horizons for at least one night. We spend so much of our time working here in the hospital, we forget there's a great big world out there. We'll have a buffet supper outside, and music so we can dance. I'd like to have a platform and lanterns put up. What do you think? Do you like the idea?"

Jason put his arms around her waist and kissed her on the temple. "I'd like it a whole lot more if we announced our engagement at the party."

"You said you would be patient and wait, Jason," she reminded him gently. "Let's wait until the fall. That will give me enough time to see if I can sort out the financial troubles we're having. Then, I'll have time to think about us."

As if to ask forgiveness for this new delay, she

raised her lips to his, yet she felt full of doubts and questions about their wedding. Was she really sure how she felt about him? Did she really love him—or was she just satisfied to let things go on the way they were? Maybe she just wanted to let things drift. Maybe she didn't want to get married at all. Jason meant a great deal to her, she knew that. She needed him and counted on his support to help her run the hospital. With him by her side, she always felt a deep sense of security, calm and reassurance. She reveled in this feeling and wanted to keep it in her life. The past was over now as far as she was concerned and life seemed good. But she had to admit to herself that she did feel troubled lately. . . .

THE FOLLOWING DAY, in the morning, Ben Aroual phoned the Foundation and asked Shannon to come to his house right away. When Shannon was called to the phone, she left her patient for a minute to talk to him. "Is Fawzia having contractions?" she asked instantly.

The banker reassured her that it had nothing to do with his daughter, but rather with his oldest grandson, Karim, who was about ten years old. He was complaining of severe stomach cramps and had been vomiting all morning.

"I'm just finishing my morning rounds. I'll be there in about half an hour," Shannon promised.

Around one o'clock, Shannon returned to the Foundation with a report on Karim's condition and joined her colleagues for lunch. "I think it's appendicitis," she explained to everyone at the table. "In my opinion it's not urgent, but I think you should drop in and see the boy, Cliff. It's up to you whether he should be operated on or not. In the meantime, I've prescribed some medication to ease his condition."

Cliff nodded silently. "Well, if you think I should make a house call, I'll get over there right away," he said quietly.

"Ben Aroual would be very grateful if you did," Shannon said. "He's opposed to an operation unless it's absolutely necessary, but he would value your professional opinion. In fact, I'd like to come with you. I wanted to see Fawzia today anyway, and she wasn't there earlier. And I didn't get a chance to talk to Ben Aroual about a couple of important matters."

Carol, who was sitting beside one of the nurses, hadn't paid much attention to Shannon's diagnosis. However, these words caught her attention immediately and, without seeming to, she looked around at her luncheon companions and covertly gauged their reactions to her sister's suggestion. Cliff agreed to her plan without comment. Divina kept her eyes fixed on her plate and Jason showed no reaction at all, his face an unreadable mask.

It was a little after two o'clock when Shannon and Cliff met in the hospital driveway. The sun was blinding, the air hot and dry.

Shannon had taken the jeep out of the garage and was just putting the top up to protect them from the white heat of the sun when Cliff joined her.

"Yassef has gone to the airport with the truck to pick up a shipment of medical supplies coming from the Red Cross," she explained. "Shall I drive or would you rather?"

"I would enjoy driving," he said quietly.

She was glad to let him take the wheel. She didn't really enjoy driving and took the jeep out herself only when it was absolutely necessary. When they were settled in the car, he drove down the driveway and out onto the street leading into town, leaving behind clouds of ocher-colored dust. There was almost no traffic: not many people came out at this time of day when the sun was high in the sky. When they got outside the walls of the hospital, the heat bore down on them and Shannon felt as if she had stepped into an inferno. There was one good thing about the heat, Cliff commented. The air was so dry you didn't perspire and end up in a totally weakened condition.

"I'm planning on giving a party to celebrate the anniversary of the hospital," Shannon announced suddenly. "I'm going to invite Ben Aroual. I hope you and your friend, Divina, will come too. I'm going to invite the rest of the staff at dinner tomorrow. There won't be any more than twelve guests from outside the hospital. It's really only a friendly little get-together."

"I would be delighted to come," Cliff replied enthusiastically.

"Divina, too?" she asked, rather probingly.

"Divina can make up her own mind," he replied. "Whether she comes or not has nothing to do with me."

"Oh, I'm sorry. I thought it did," Shannon blurted

out, and then was suddenly appalled at her lack of tact. *Why on earth did I say that,* she thought. *It's none of my business.*

"What makes you say that?" he asked, as he took his foot off the accelerator and turned to look at her.

"Well, to tell you truth, I don't really know. It was just an impression I had, that's all," she replied, blushing with embarrassment. Much to her relief, he seemed to accept her explanation and turned his eyes back to the road.

"Well, to tell you the truth, I don't really know. It was just an impression I had, that's all," she replied, Now, do I turn right here or keep going straight through?"

"Take the first street to your right. Follow the river for a couple of blocks, then turn down the next street to your left."

Cliff lapsed into silence again. Shannon decided to take a chance and ask him another question. "Have I offended you?"

"Not in the least."

"I don't want to pry. It's just that we're a close group at the hospital and we're always very open with one another whenever possible. So please, don't be angry with us if we seem to be overly curious about your private life. We're not really being nosy—it's just that we care about the people we work with and want to help out in any way we can. Our curiosity is really a sign of interest and affection. I hope you can take it in that spirit. Don't you believe me?" she asked, when he smiled increduously.

"Your group does seem close and harmonious," he

commented adroitly ignoring her reference to his private life. "But I've never come across a totally altruistic group of people, have you? I mean, it's almost impossible for people to live together without some kind of tension or difficulty. Each person brings his faults as well as his strengths into a group, so there can't help but be antagonisms, internal rivalries, arguments, that kind of thing."

Shannon sensed he was referring to her relationship with Carol and he immediately confirmed her suspicion. "I guess what I'm getting at is that I've noticed that you and your stepsister aren't on the best of terms."

"That may be true, but I'm not trying to hide it from anyone. And besides, it doesn't have anything to do with the rest of the staff. They get on quite well together."

"Well, I'm glad everything is working out so well," he replied as he looked around the neighborhood. "I recognize this area. Ben Aroual's house isn't far from here, is it?"

"That's right. You've got a good memory," she remarked.

Before long, the jeep reached the gates that stood open at the edge of Ben Aroual's property. They drove up the winding driveway to the basin of lotus flowers and stopped in front of the house.

While Aroual accompanied Cliff to his grandson's room, Shannon dropped in for a quick visit with Fawzia.

When Cliff entered the boy's room, he found the child stretched out on a couch surrounded by his

relatives. Karim seemed much better and his fever
was down. Cliff confirmed Shannon's diagnosis. It
had been a severe attack of appendicitis but, for the
moment, an operation wasn't necessary. He went on
to explain that if another attack occurred, Karim
would have to be brought to the hospital for an
appendectomy. Ben Aroual and the child's parents
listened carefully to his advice and promised to do
exactly as he said.

When the two men returned to the living room,
Shannon was waiting for them. It was the same room
in which the older man had received them on their
first visit to his home, and once again he served them
dark Turkish coffee and delicious little cakes.

After enquiring about Karim's health and in-
forming Aroual that his daughter was doing very
well, Shannon said she wished to talk to him about
the Foundation. When Cliff made a move to leave,
she asked him to stay.

"Please don't go, Cliff. You're an important
member of the staff now, and you should know
exactly how things stand with regard to the
hospital.

"As time goes by," she said, turning to look at
Aroual, "I realize only too well that my grandfather
was right. His worries were based on cold, hard
facts. Our financial situation is very bad. In spite of
the generosity of you and your friends, and even
with our constant efforts to bring in more money, we
hardly have enough to cover our expenses and the
salaries of our staff. We're all overloaded with work,
but I just haven't got the money to hire extra staff."

"I know what you're up against," Ben Aroual replied immediately, "and I'm going to inform the governor about your financial status right away. Also I intend to continue helping as much as I can. However, I'm afraid my intervention won't be enough. The political situation right now is quite confusing, and I don't know how much I can do under the circumstances."

"You've done so much for us already—I can't tell you how grateful I am. I was wondering how I, personally, could improve matters. I thought I would go to Cairo around the first of October, before the next meeting of the Health and Welfare Committee, and ask to see the chairman. Do you think that would be a good idea?"

"It might. You would want to approach it carefully, though."

"Do you think it would help if you signed the petition I'm going to submit? Your signature would lend more weight to the petition and to the report that goes with it."

"I was going to suggest the very same myself," Aroual replied enthusiastically. "Go ahead and draft your letter for the petition, Shannon. I'll be delighted to sign it, and I'm sure the governor will be, too. I'll have it approved by some local officials here, as well. I think this will help a great deal, and increase your credibility."

Delighted at his generous and concerned response, Shannon looked at the older man and smiled gratefully. "I can't tell you how much I appreciate all your help. You've been very kind."

"Going to Cairo to present your case to the committee is an excellent idea," he responded approvingly.

For the next few minutes, the three of them continued to discuss the various problems that cropped up at the hospital during the course of a day's work and tried to find answers to some of their more pressing problems. They managed to come up with a few suggestions, but these were only stop-gap measures and didn't provide any permanent solutions. If the hospital was going to work smoothly and efficiently, they desperately needed that subsidy from the government.

Toward the end of their discussion, Shannon asked Ben Aroual to her anniversary party. The older man was touched by her invitation and graciously accepted. Around seven o'clock Shannon and Cliff said goodbye to their host and took their leave.

After their relaxing visit in the cool interior of the banker's home, the heat didn't seem so intolerable when they stepped outside and walked toward the jeep.

"Do you know the old city at all?" Shannon asked as they got into the well-worn vehicle.

"I've only been there once, but I didn't stay long. Why?"

"Well, I have a house call to make there. Would you like to come along?"

"Well . . . I'd like to, but I really should get back. I have a lot of work to do," he replied reluctantly.

"Come on, get in," she said persuasively. "This won't take us long."

"All right, but I think you'd better take the wheel this time. I don't know my way around," he replied.

As they made their way toward the old city, Cliff brought up Shannon's projected visit to Cairo. "I was thinking about your trip just now and I have a suggestion that might help. An old friend of mine works in Cairo. We've always been very close and still keep in touch. Strangely enough, he just happens to be the nephew of the present Minister of Health."

"Really?" she exclaimed.

"I'm pretty sure he could get you an interview with his uncle."

"It would be wonderful if he could," she murmured, looking at Cliff, her eyes bright with hope.

"Hey, watch out!" he exclaimed with a mock look of horror on his face. "You almost ran over that poor old donkey."

"I'm used to driving through crowds of donkeys and camels," she replied, bursting out laughing. "It's not as dangerous as it looks."

"Well, are you interested in my idea?" he asked, once they were through the congestion.

"More than I can tell you," she replied excitedly. "I'm very grateful to you for thinking of it and for caring enough to intercede with your friend on my behalf."

"When do you think you'll be going to Cairo?"

"Around the middle of September. In the meantime, Jason is going to help me draw up a detailed report on the Foundation. Once I'm finished with that, Ben Aroual will get the signatures I need."

"How would you feel if I came to Cairo with you?"

he asked suddenly. "It would certainly be more practical. We could talk to my friend together, that way."

It was an excellent idea. Strategically, it would be the right thing to do, but for some unknown reason, Shannon suddenly felt uneasy. "Well, I, uh . . ." she stammered.

"Are you afraid people might talk?" he asked, sensing her discomfort.

They were approaching the poor section of the city. The roads were beginning to narrow and there were all kinds of vehicles crowding the twisting streets: horse-drawn carts, hand carts, old bicycles. The traffic was so heavy it was difficult to keep the car moving. Shannon turned her attention to maneuvering the jeep safely through the throngs of people, but still managed to keep the conversation going. "What do you mean, people would talk?"

"Well, someone might not like the idea of our traveling together," he remarked easily, his clear blue eyes gazing intently at her profile.

She didn't dare look at him, and for a moment she had the uneasy impression that, if she asked the question on the tip of her tongue, she would definitely be playing with fire. But she blurted it out before she could stop herself. "You mean someone like Divina, for example?"

"I was thinking of Jason, actually," he said evenly. "You're unofficially engaged, aren't you?"

Without thinking, Shannon was instantly on the defensive. "Did someone tell you that? Who was it?" she asked.

"No—no one in particular."

"You're being rather vague, aren't you?"

"Well, since I didn't go out of my way to find out, I don't feel it would be right to reveal my source."

Shannon quickly realized he wasn't going to answer her questions. *It doesn't really matter*, she told herself. One of these days, she would have to come out and make an official announcement. After all, if everyone knew, her continued secrecy was bound to seem ridiculous. She knew her secret was safe for a little while longer, but time was running out.

"For the moment, nothing is official between Jason and me. We date, that's all. But that's beside the point. Business is business, and this trip to Cairo is a very important matter. I can't afford to make any mistakes where the hospital is concerned—too much depends upon it. So . . . insofar as business goes, I'm quite free to go where I please with whomever I please. If you are, too, I think it would be wise to have you come along with me to Cairo."

"That's settled, then: we'll go together. I'm sure you'll like my friend. He's a marvelous doctor and quite a remarkable person. He went to school in Paris but he's also visited the States. He's quite a mixture, actually. His father is Egyptian, his uncle is the Minister of Health in Cairo and his mother is an English librarian."

"How interesting. How did he manage such a history?"

"Easy. Two people just fell in love and surmounted all the obstacles and racial prejudices that stood in their way. It's a beautiful story, really, and Ari Khalam is the result."

Shannon envied a couple whose love was strong enough to triumph over all difficulties. She wondered again if what she felt for Jason was love. Did the feeling she had for him have that kind of strength and endurance? This was the second time in as many days that she'd asked herself that kind of question. She ignored the feeling of uncertainty that welled up in her each time she examined her feeling for Jason and hurriedly told herself she needed his tender and kindly presence in her life and would be lost without him.

She stopped the jeep at the end of a narrow street lined with mud-walled buildings that housed several families. All the houses in this neighborhood were the same. Many of them didn't have a roof and were covered with palm leaves, gunny bags or sheet metal to keep out the blazing sun. In the midst of the semi-squalor stood a glistening white mosque with its lattice-work minaret soaring against the sky.

A foul odor rose from a heap of garbage on the corner: a mangy cat was scrounging for scraps of food. Half-naked children, playing noisily in spite of the incredible heat, interrupted their game to follow the visitors, begging for pennies or a few candies. Shannon had come prepared: she gave the children handfuls of candies as she walked through the streets.

She stopped in front of a dirty little shack. "I delivered the last child of the woman we're going to see. I brought some powdered milk and some vitamins for the mother. We've persuaded her to keep nursing, but we have to keep her healthy enough to feed her baby."

Cliff followed her into the house. It had two rooms with hard-packed earth floors and rough walls.

In the first room, the baby was lying on a mat near his mother, who was sitting on the floor. Two other children of about five and six were playing in one corner. When the woman saw Shannon, she smiled and said a few words in Arabic.

Shannon handed her the provisions she had brought and took the newborn baby in her arms to show Cliff.

"He's only two months old," she said softly.

The child didn't even look one month old and his little face was pitifully thin. During Shannon's brief examination, the baby woke up but didn't cry out or make a sound. Shannon smiled and stroked the baby's cheek fondly.

"His general health is okay but he's seriously undernourished, and he isn't clean. I wonder if she's been giving him water, too; he's dehydrated," Shannon noticed. "His mother has to nurse him a lot more than she is doing. Also, she should be bringing the baby to the hospital once a month so we can examine him regularly and explain to her how to care for him. We would also be able to provide her with the supplements she needs."

Shannon then made her suggestions to the mother, who seemed relieved and impressed by her words. "I think she's going to come to the hospital tomorrow," Shannon announced. "I've asked her to do this before but she's never come."

"I didn't know you spoke Arabic," Cliff said, surprised.

"I don't, really. Just a few words. However, I did manage to make myself understood."

"Is she married?"

"Yes, she is. Her husband doesn't get home until late at night. After the dam was finished, he lost his job and he works on a farm outside the city now. But his health is getting worse each year. Like most of the population, he's got bilharzia, and it slowly takes its toll. And, so far, there is little that can be done."

A few moments later, as they were driving along the wide, clean streets of the new city, Cliff turned to her and said, "You know, I've never seen this kind of poverty. I understand now why your grandfather created the Mallison Foundation. It's work like this that makes a person feel worthwhile."

Shannon said nothing but turned to look at him. She thanked him with a brilliant smile.

Chapter 8

The night of the party finally arrived. Besides the staff of the Foundation, Shannon had invited several well known personalities from Aswan. Among the guests were the British director of the Botanical Gardens, two French archaeologists, the head of a German import-export firm and his wife, Ben Aroual and some local politicians.

The day before the party, Shannon had made some tentative overtures toward Carol in the hopes of taking a few steps, no matter how small, toward narrowing the gap between them. "Would you like to share the role of hostess with me tomorrow?" she had asked.

Carol hadn't been able to sidestep her sister's invitation. She had reluctantly agreed to help host the anniversary party. She seemed to like the idea of all the attention, but Shannon knew she would try to avoid doing any work.

She had shrugged philosophically; at least she had enlisted her stepsister's alliance to a certain extent, and she was pleased with her effort at diplomacy.

A half-hour before the guests would begin arriving, Shannon, dressed for the occasion, was making last-minute preparations. As Nadah walked back and forth from the kitchen, Shannon was telling her how she wanted everything done. She looked beautiful in a silver lamé gown that fell in soft folds over her slender hips. Her hair, which was usually piled on top of her head in a bun, fell loosely down her back in big, golden curls.

Carol, too, was ready for the guests. She was wearing a shiny black and purple dress that emphasized her figure. She opened the door of her room and stepped out into the hall just as the first knock on the door was heard.

Jason was the first to arrive. He was obviously looking forward to the evening and its festivities.

"You look marvelous," he exclaimed, taking in Shannon's appearance with an admiring glance. He pulled her into his arms, kissing her passionately and deeply. Carol, leaning languidly against the door, took in the tender love scene without glancing away.

"Jason, please, you're messing my hair," Shannon protested.

Carol took a deep breath and sighed loudly. She was leaning against the door jamb, her hand set provocatively on her hip.

Jason turned with surprise. "Carol! Have you added being a Peeping Tom to your list of

pleasures?" he teased. "Would you like to see some
more?" He grabbed Shannon again, but she backed
off in puzzled surprise.

"What's going on around here, anyway?" she
asked. "You two play whatever games you want. I've
got a thousand and one chores to finish."

"Play games with him?" Carol laughed. "Who
would want to?"

"I was just going to tell you how ravishing you
look," Jason commented adroitly.

"*Ravishing.* Now that's a good word, Jason." She
threw back her head and giggled, her figure exposed
to full advantage.

"Umm . . . yes. I see what you mean," Jason said.

Just then Shannon passed them and Jason grabbed
her by the waist, then held her wrists and pinned her
to the wall.

"Jason! What's come over you, anyway?"

"I'm just getting the party going, that's all. And
this is what happens when you let your hair down."
He was kissing her between his words and pressing
his body against hers.

"Let me go, Jason," Shannon protested, flushed
with embarrassment. Carol was standing directly in
front of her, steely eyes taking in every detail.
"You're not being nice. Carol's watching."

"Carol loves it. Don't you, Carol?" he whispered,
before pressing his lips against Shannon's and kissing
her deeply.

With a smile he released Shannon, who was both
bewildered and offended. She didn't know quite how
to take what had just happened. But she didn't have

time to dwell on it. Tonight was her night, and she wasn't going to let anything upset her. Without a word, she turned and continued her business.

Jason turned expectantly but Carol, too, was gone.

A few moments later, summoning all her self-control, Shannon assumed a bright, gracious smile and began greeting the guests as they arrived. Before long she was serving drinks and hors d'oeuvres and making small talk as she circulated among the assembled guests.

The party went extremely well. It had been too long since everyone had gotten together just for the sake of a good time. The stereo was set up so that the speakers could be heard out on the lawn, where a table laden with delicacies from the White Nile stood under a string of festive lights. Near the table was a platform especially made for dancing, and in no time at all the square was jammed with happy couples dancing their hearts out in the cool breeze of the summer night. The quieter groups gathered inside, where there was food and drinks and good conversation.

After midnight, when everyone was starting to feel they had danced more than ever before in one night, Shannon's voice rang out over the hum of conversation.

"Friends, may I have your attention please? For the past few days, there has been an exhibition of trained snakes and other scary things at the Hotel Isis. I asked the gentleman in charge if he could come here this evening to give us a private showing. He was kind enough to reschedule his last performance to tomorrow, just so he could be with us here tonight. Please give him a warm welcome and enjoy the show."

The guests immediately found their way to the chairs that had been set up in a semicircle at the far end of the room. An Egyptian with dark eyes and a white turban, his face sporting a well-trimmed dark beard, walked into the room carrying several delicately woven bags and a few metallic boxes.

As he opened the bags one by one he held up several poisonous snakes of all colors and sizes, displaying the creatures with great poise and expertise to his captivated but slightly fearful audience. From the last bag he took a huge cobra, which he held up with both arms for everyone to see.

The climax of the show was a fight to the death between two deadly scorpions. Fascinated, everyone leaned forward and watched the two insects eye one another before throwing themselves into mortal combat. The fight didn't last long. In a few seconds, one of the scorpions dropped dead from the fatal sting of its opponent. Shannon watched the spectacle with horror, glancing up occasionally to gauge the reactions of her guests. Some of the more squeamish spectators were looking at their feet, she noticed, but her stepsister was on the edge of her chair, obviously enjoying the combat.

As the guests applauded enthusiastically, the man smiled, bowed graciously and left the room.

The party didn't thin out until after two o'clock, and judging from the peals of laughter and warm feelings on everyone's part, it was a tremendous success. Most of the guests attributed the warm, relaxing atmosphere to Shannon, who was able to put people at ease and make them feel welcomed. Perhaps it was the fact that she loved these people, and that her feelings for them showed, that started the party off on the right foot. In every respect, it was an evening to be remembered fondly.

Finally, only Shannon, Jason and Carol remained in the house, surrounded by the debris of a festive evening. Shannon had completely forgotten her momentary annoyance with Jason earlier in the evening. She was filled with the euphoria and contented exhaustion that comes with having worked very hard and having everything go perfectly as a result.

Feeling exuberant, she was bantering with Jason in the kitchen. Jason was teasing her, demanding what it was she and Cliff were talking about every time he looked around. Shannon pointed out that Jason had a fairly nice time in that respect himself, considering Divina, Ella, Hilda and Beth. "And then how about . . ." she began, but he pulled her to him with a laugh and embraced her warmly, tenderly nuzzling her in the crook of the neck. "Umm," Shannon crooned with a giggle, her golden hair falling in curls over her shoulders.

Carol was sitting sullenly on the couch, smoking a cigarette and sipping her drink. Abruptly she stood up, announced that she was exhausted and went directly to her room. She quickly got undressed and stretched out on her bed.

In the living room, a slightly subdued Shannon put

a record on the stereo. The music drifted softly over the garden, lending an atmosphere of enchantment to the cool Egyptian night.

THE NEXT EVENING AFTER DINNER, Carol waited until Shannon went back to the hospital to work on the report she was preparing for the government in Cairo, then she quietly slipped out of the house. She hurried quickly toward the servants' quarters where Yassef lived and knocked lightly on his door. Almost immediately, Yassef was standing in front of her, a questioning look in his dark eyes.

"I want to go into town, Yassef," she said as soon as he'd opened the door. "I'll give you fifty dollars if you take me."

"Does Shannon know about this?" he asked, obviously tempted by her offer.

"No, and she doesn't have to," Carol replied calmly. "I know she doesn't like me going out at night but I promised some friends of mine I would drop by and see them before they left, and they're sailing for England tomorrow. I won't stay long."

"I think it would be better if I asked first," the handyman insisted stubbornly.

"Listen, Yassef, either you accept the money I'm offering you and take me into town or I'm going alone. Take your choice," she announced crisply, taking a ten dollar bill out of her pocket and waving it under his nose.

Torn between his greed and his fear of Shannon's disapproval if she found out, Yassef stood in the doorway in an agony of hesitation. "You shouldn't go into town alone at night," he said.

"Okay, then, take the money and come with me," she replied quickly.

He hesitated for a few seconds longer, then gave in and nodded quietly. He took the money, put it in his pocket and walked with her to the garage. As he was opening the garage doors, he turned to Carol and said, "You're going to have to help me push the car out to the main road. I can't start the motor until we get to the hill. Someone might hear us."

The car wasn't hard to push and when they reached the main road, they jumped in and drove off.

"Take me to the New Waterfall Hotel," she said firmly.

They drove in silence and in ten minutes they had reached the hotel.

"Drive around the block a couple of times and wait for me out here," Carol said crisply. "I won't be gone long," she added over her shoulder, as she disappeared into the lobby.

Rapidly, she crossed the lobby unobserved, reached the lounge and walked into the inner courtyard. Behind the swimming pool there was a service entrance that led to a narrow, badly lit back alley. Quickly, she ran across the grass and disappeared out the door. A few minutes later, she walked calmly into the lobby of the Hotel Isis.

The man she was looking for had finished with the first part of the show and was just starting the dramatic finale: the battle of the scorpions. Carol slipped quietly in among the small group of tourists who were crowded around, avidly watching the brief but deadly struggle of the two giant insects. When it was over and the crowd had dispersed, Carol walked up to the man who was slowly gathering up his containers of deadly cargo.

"Would you be willing to sell me two or three of your scorpions? I would pay a good price for them."

He turned slowly and looked at her somberly. She stood quietly waiting for his answer.

"Scorpions?" he asked. "Don't you realize these insects are dangerous? They could kill you."

"Yes, I know."

"Why do you want them?" he asked her abruptly.

"I'm a teacher in a mission school. I want to show the scorpions to the children so they can learn to recognize them, to avoid getting stung."

"I have to leave Aswan tomorrow morning. Otherwise I would have been delighted to come and give a demonstration. I could let you have two, if you like. Both are extremely dangerous—one can kill, so you could put on a fight for your students. But don't forget to kill the victor."

"Right, I won't," Carol replied. "How much do you want for them?"

"Fifty dollars each."

"Fifty dollars!" she exclaimed. "You're kidding. That's far too expensive. Don't you realize that the mission schools are supported by charities and only have a little money to spend on things like this?"

"That may be so," he replied quietly, "but I can't let these insects go any cheaper. I paid a lot for them myself and they'll be hard to replace. They're not easy to find."

"I'll give you fifty dollars for both of them," she bargained.

"I can't accept an offer like that. I'll be losing money. Seventy-five for the two of them."

"Fifty."

"That's impossible. I would rather keep them and not take any money at all."

"As you wish."

As she turned to leave, he stopped her. "All right, then."

The man picked up one of his empty boxes and began filling it with sand. "It looks like I'm beaten," he sighed, "but Allah will reward me for being so generous."

Carol stood quietly, anxiously waiting for him to finish. With small wooden pincers, he picked up a black scorpion and put it in one compartment of the box. Then he picked up another, a sand-colored one, and put it in a different compartment.

"The black one is deadly and can kill you. The other one can make you very sick and his sting is painful but it won't kill you. Be sure to remember this—your life, as well as the safety of your students, will depend on it."

Carol nodded silently as he closed the box carefully and accepted the money she had ready for him.

A few minutes later she was back at the car where Yassef was dozing at the wheel. She touched him gently on the shoulder and he awoke with a start. "Okay, let's go," she said quietly.

Chapter 9

When the car was safely back in the garage once more, Carol hurried noiselessly across the hospital grounds to the house. Quietly, she tiptoed toward Shannon's bedroom, which was next to hers. She noticed that her sister had left her door half open to allow Pepsie to come and go as he pleased. Shannon was in bed, asleep.

Carol tiptoed down the hall to her own room. She rummaged through her drawers until she found an empty bottle and a long pair of tweezers. Sitting on the bed, she put these items on the bedside table beside the little box with some sense of ceremony.

When she lifted the lid of the box, she saw the scorpions lying motionless inside. Slowly, she took the tweezers in her trembling hand, picked up one of the scorpions and placed it in the bottle. Then she went back out into the hall, stopped in front of her sister's door and looked in. Shannon was sleeping soundly, her golden hair spread out on the pillow, reflecting the bright moonlight streaming in through the windows. Carol slipped into the room and walked silently and slowly toward the bed. She emptied the bottle onto the sheet and backed toward the door, fascinated by the slowly moving black form that was creeping, its deadly little stinger curved and taut, toward Shannon's naked shoulder. With a violent shudder, Carol turned and left the room.

When she reached her bedroom, she made sure the box containing the other scorpion was closed tightly and hid it under the cushion of one of her big armchairs.

After making sure the door to her room was securely shut, Carol undressed and lay down, pulling the bedspread over her head.

WHEN DAWN STREAKED THE EASTERN SKY, Carol was still lying rigidly and painfully awake. At seven, Nadah arrived at the house and began opening the shutters. Carol could hear her talking to Pepsie and busying herself around the kitchen. Before long, the comforting aroma of coffee and fresh bread flooded through the house.

Suddenly Carol heard the door of Shannon's closet creak and the sound of her curtains being pulled open. After a night of deadly silence, the morning was alive with the sounds of life and a new day was beginning.

Shannon was alive. She had escaped the horrible death that had stalked her in the darkness. Carol buried her head in the pillows and sobbed.

WHEN SHANNON WALKED into the dining room at
eight o'clock, she didn't expect to find Carol waiting
for her at the breakfast table. It was only on rare
occasions that her stepsister was up at this hour of
the morning, and during the last few weeks she had
hardly shown up at all.

With a sudden rush of nostalgia, Shannon thought
back to the mornings when her grandfather was still
alive, when Carol and she had still been friends.
Mornings had always been the best time of the day in
their little family. They had been happy, full of life
and interesting plans for the coming day. Suppress-
ing a sigh, Shannon had a quick cup of coffee and a
piece of toast and then left for the hospital, unaware
of her stepsister watching furtively through the
window as she walked across the garden toward the
hospital.

Secure in the knowledge that Shannon had left the
house for the day and that Nadah would be busy
cleaning up in the kitchen for a while, Carol put on
some thick-soled shoes and slipped noiselessly down
the hall into her sister's room. Without wasting a
second, she began a methodical but careful search.
There was no trace of the scorpion anywhere. In
vain, she shook the drapes and the sheets and looked
under the pillows and mattress. Trying to control her
rising panic, she bent down and looked under the
bed, the table and the two chairs.

Then, glancing up, she spotted the deadly creature
in the folds of the mosquito netting that covered the
window.

Without a moment's hesitation, Carol ran over to

the window and shook the scorpion free. When it feel to the floor, she crushed it under the thick sole of her shoe. With a sigh of relief, she picked up the harmless body of the dead insect, took it to the bathroom and flushed it away.

Then she returned to her room and collapsed with relief in one of the big armchairs. Almost immediately, she felt a sharp sting and leaped to her feet, screaming in pain. She looked around the room frantically, and caught sight of the second scorpion, even now trying to scurry away out of the room.

In spite of the pain in her thigh, Carol killed the insect with one thud of her heel. The she cleaned up the sand that had spilled out on the chair when she had tipped the box over. She also carefully hid the box before calling Nadah for help.

Alerted by the scream from Carol's bedroom Nadah appeared almost instantly.

"Go quick," Carol cried. "Get Jason. He's probably still at home. Tell him I've just been stung by a scorpion."

"A scorpion?" Nadah echoed, a terrified expression on her face. "You mean right here in your room?"

"Yes, yes. Now go quickly."

Nadah ran out of the room and Carol heard her footsteps echoing into the distance. She hoped Nadah could reach Jason before he left for the hospital. Her leg was becoming stiff and very painful.

In a few minutes, Cliff came running into the room. He found Carol sitting on her bed, her hands clutching at her naked thigh.

"Jason is with a patient but I was next door. How did this happen?" he asked, as he inspected the mark on her leg. "Where is the scorpion?"

"Over there," Carol said, motioning to the lifeless body of the insect. "It stung me when I sat in my chair."

Cliff examined the scorpion. "You're all right," he said gravely. "It's not one of the deadly kind. But how did it get in here with all that mosquito netting at the window? It seems impossible."

"Maybe this morning when Nadah opened all the windows to air the house," Carol suggested, thinking feverishly.

"But how did it get into the bedroom?" he persisted.

"There's already been a scorpion in the house. There was one a couple of weeks ago," Nadah explained. "We got Yassef to come and kill it. But it wasn't like this one."

"Your leg is starting to swell up badly," Cliff commented. "We've got to get you to the hospital right away. I'll drain the wound and apply some disinfectant, then give you an injection."

Carol was shivering violently, and when she tried to stand up she almost fainted. Without a moment's hesitation, Cliff picked her up in his strong arms and looked down at her gravely. "Don't worry, Carol, you're going to be all right," he reassured her. "You'll be in a lot of pain for a while, but in a few days you'll be back to normal," he added kindly, his voice unusually soft and gentle.

Burning tears of fear sprang to her eyes as she rested her head dizzily against his shoulder.

After treating Carol for the scorpion sting, Cliff took her back to the house and then went immediately to find Shannon. Very briefly, he told her what had happened, including Carol's report of how the scorpion had gotten into the house. "You've got to take more precautions from now on," he said firmly. "Get Yassef to check all the mosquito netting and have the gardeners spray the garden so there's no chance those things can multiply and overrun the place."

Shannon nodded quickly and said she would see to it right away.

"I think you should go and see Carol," Cliff continued. "She seems shaken by the incident. She's very frightened and quite upset."

When Shannon walked into Carol's room, the younger woman was sleeping fitfully, her forehead beaded with small drops of perspiration, her cheeks flushed. Shannon didn't want to wake her and slipped quietly out of the room and went back to the hospital. Before she returned to the maternity ward, however, she dropped in to see Cliff and told him Carol was feverish. He said he'd like to look in on her later that morning.

"I'll try to join you back at the house around noon," Shannon assured him.

When Cliff got to the house a little before noon, Nadah greeted him anxiously. "I was just on my way to get you," she said quickly. "I've looked in on

Carol several times this morning. She's very agitated and is saying all kinds of strange things. I'm frightened."

When Cliff saw Carol, he realized she was feverish and delirious. He was surprised she was having such a violent reaction and immediately gave her a sedative injection to calm her down. He scribbled a few words on a piece of paper, handed it to Nadah and asked her to deliver it to Shannon at the hospital. Then he sat down and waited quietly by Carol's bedside.

In the dim light of her room, Carol began muttering disconnected words. Cliff leaned over and tried to hear what she was saying.

"You have to die, Shannon . . . fifty dollars . . . . Look, the scorpion is over there on the bed," she mumbled as she tossed and turned, caught in the grip of a horrible nightmare, her pretty face tense and drawn.

Cliff stood up slowly. Why was Carol talking about Shannon dying when she had been the one who had been stung?

Carol began thrashing around on the bed, moaning and whimpering like a child. Cliff gently took her wrist and checked her pulse. It was very rapid. Before long, the sedative began to take effect and eased the frenzied dreams. Slowly, Carol began to relax. Cliff pulled the sheet back up over her and sat down again beside the bed.

Shannon's sudden arrival broke in on his thoughts. Still somewhat preoccupied, he got up to greet her.

"I think she should have another antitoxin shot and something for her fever," he explained. "She's really sick."

Shannon took one look at Carol and nodded. She took a washcloth from the basin of cold water beside the bed, wrung it out and began wiping her stepsister's feverish brow. "She's delirious. This isn't a normal reaction," she said.

"No, it isn't. But everything's going to be all right. I've never seen anything quite like this. At first she was in a severe state of shock, highly emotional. Her leg swelled up very quickly, but that's quite normal. I'll keep an eye on her for a while to make sure there're no complications."

As Cliff gave Carol another antitoxin shot, Shannon wiped her brow with the cold cloth once again.

"We should just let her rest now," Cliff said quietly. "Ask Nadah to come and sit by her. Tell her not to leave her for a minute. If Carol starts getting agitated again, she must let me know immediately."

Cliff turned abruptly and left the room. A few minutes later, after repeating his instructions to Nadah, Shannon returned to the hospital.

FORTY-EIGHT HOURS LATER, Carol's fever finally broke. Her nightmares had left her drained and exhausted, and she stayed in bed for several more days.

On the fourth day, Shannon visited her stepsister on a mission of peace. She brought Carol a special gift. Unwrapping it tenderly, she handed it to Carol, who was still too weak to sit up in bed. It was a tiny, gold-colored statue of a woman, about the size of Carol's hand. The arms were outstretched in a graceful motion that was both protective and inviting.

"Who is it?" Carol asked.

"It's the Egyptian goddess Selket. She protects against scorpion stings—that's her speciality. See that thing on her head. That's a scorpion."

"Ugh. Just what I need. Where did you get it?"

"Oh . . . I've had it for awhile, but I figured you needed it now. I hope you like it—I've been very fond of her."

"Yes . . . . sure I do. Thank you," Carol said weakly, staring blankly at the magical statue in her hand.

CAUGHT UP IN THE DEMANDS of his work, Cliff almost forgot about the strange words Carol had muttered in her delirium. Shannon, too, was busier than ever. It was almost as if she wanted to fill her life with work so there would be no room for any unwanted emotions that might arise and overwhelm her well-ordered life.

It was taking Carol a long time to get over the psychological shock she had sustained. Although she was physically better, she continued to appear depressed. She had resumed her passive way of life now, and her relationship with Shannon was only slightly improved. Shannon was doing all she could to make friends again and was being much warmer to

Carol than she had been in a long time. But Carol was not responding.

The month of August passed uneventfully. The heat was almost unbearable, the sky like a piece of burning sheet metal, reflecting the dazzling light of the blazing sun. Once in a while, the sky would cloud over momentarily and everyone's spirits would rise as they contemplated the possibility of a cool, refreshing rain. But the rain never came.

As soon as Shannon finished her report on the activities of the Foundation for the government in Cairo, she set the date for her departure and began planning the trip.

Three of them were going: Shannon, Jason and Cliff. She had given the matter some thought, and it was with an inexplicable sense of relief that she had decided to persuade Jason to come to Cairo with her. It hadn't been easy. "But look at how important the hospital is to you," she had argued. "And you know so much. It would be a big help—something in our favor—if you came, too." Finally he agreed and Shannon gratefully thanked him with a kiss.

But now she found herself in the trying situation of having to tell Jason that Cliff would be accompanying them on their trip. She was worried that Cliff would be annoyed, or might find the situation strange. Shannon decided to allow the matter to slip for a few days; then she would do something about it

Both Jason and Cliff had been working very hard. Thanks to the two of them, she had finished the report a little sooner than expected and was grateful to them both for giving up hours of their time to help her make the report as detailed and concise as possible.

Ben Aroual sent her a letter, signed by himself and the governor of the province, that was addressed to the most influential members of the Health and Welfare Committee in Cairo. He also mailed her a list of all those people who were in favor of a permanent government subsidy for the Foundation. Armed with these documents, her own report and Cliff's promise to help when they got to Cairo, Shannon hoped to triumph over the indifference and inertia of the bureaucracy once and for all.

"When we get back, maybe you'll have time to think a little more about us," Jason remarked when they were alone one evening.

Shannon didn't feel like getting involved in that particular discussion and tried to keep the conversation light. "I hope so, too, but we still have a lot to do. For now, all I can think about is that meeting with the people in Cairo."

When Shannon finally told Jason that Cliff was going to Cairo with them and had offered to set up an interview for her with the Minister of Health, he appeared to take the news in a calm, unruffled fashion.

Shannon looked at him closely, wondering if his calm was only a facade.

"Anyway, if I fail this time, it's curtains for the Foundation," she told Jason quietly. "But if we succeed, we'll owe a lot to Cliff Sinclair."

Since their last visit with Ben Aroual, Shannon and Cliff had not gone into town together, but their work at the Foundation kept them in constant contact. A friendship had begun to grow up between them, a friendship Shannon didn't discuss with anyone. And yet, despite the fact that they were on more intimate terms than before, Cliff was still very reserved about his private life and surrounded himself in mystery.

Just like Divina, Shannon often thought. Almost in spite of herself, Shannon kept hoping to discover some kind of hidden pact between Divina and Cliff but no information came to light. At dinner, Shannon often sat with Cliff, and she noticed he was more open and talkative when Divina wasn't there. Why did he feel more at ease when that silent, withdrawn girl was absent, she wondered? She remembered Cliff saying that he and Divina weren't even friends. At times she believed him; at other times, she felt swamped by nagging doubts.

Shannon was aware that she asked herself more and more questions about Cliff's past, and she sensed the beginnings of some unknown danger to her well-ordered life. To escape the issue, she threw herself heart and soul into her work. She was becoming obsessed with the man, she thought impatiently. The days passed in a frenzy of preparation and hospital work.

The day before they were to leave for Cairo, Cliff came to her office in the late afternoon to check on a few last-minute details. Business taken care of, he sat down for a chat.

"You know, Shannon, I'm really looking forward to this trip. In fact, this little break in my work is exactly what the doctor ordered. I feel like I haven't had a vacation in a hundred years—a trip to Cairo is the perfect solution."

"I'm much too worried about the outcome of this whole business to relax for a minute," Shannon replied anxiously.

"Please, don't think I'm not taking this trip seriously," Cliff interjected, looking at her gravely. "On the contrary, I'm very concerned about the success of your mission, and I sincerely hope the Egyptian government finally realizes the good work your grandfather started here and will support it wholeheartedly. Is Jason coming with us?" he asked suddenly. "I believe you said he might be interested in joining us."

"Yes, he's coming. He thinks it would be better all around if he stayed in Aswan and looked after things here at the hospital, but I talked him into coming. But I know he feels we would do just fine without him."

Cliff shot her a piercing glance but said nothing. After a brief silence he stood up, said goodbye and left the office.

THE NEXT MORNING AT seven o'clock, Jason was in the garage with Cliff and Shannon. Yassef, who was driving them to the airport, backed the car out of the garage and helped them with the luggage. Once they were seated, Shannon turned and smiled at Jason. She leaned over and gave him a quick kiss.

Jason looked at her with surprise. He was unaccustomed to her showing affection, especially in front of anyone.

As Yassef started up the driveway, Nadah came running out of the house. "There's a woman on the phone for Dr. Wilfred," she said in a rush. "She says it's very important."

Jason looked puzzled. "What could that be about?" he muttered, climbing out of the car. "I'll only be a second," he called back apologetically.

Shannon and Cliff sat uncomfortably in the car, waiting for Jason to return. Shannon felt like a nervous teenager. Shouldn't she move to the front seat where Jason had been sitting? It hardly seemed appropriate, since he would be returning immediately. Yet the pressure of Cliff's body against hers through her thin summer clothes made her uncomfortable.

"I wonder what this phone call could be about," she mumbled awkwardly, shifting in her seat. She was afraid to look at Cliff. She had come to know his disarming blue eyes all too well.

Just then Jason came running up to the car. "Look, I don't know how to tell you this, but . . . I'm going to have to stay. One of my patients is in very bad shape, and . . . ."

"Who?" Shannon asked.

"I'm afraid you wouldn't know him. He's from out of town and I only saw him for the first time yesterday. I'll explain when you get back. But go! You've got a plane to catch. Have a good trip," he said briefly, extending his hand. "Okay, Yassef, you'd better get going."

Shannon laid a restraining hand on Yassef's arm. "Wait a minute, please, Yassef," she said. Blushing

furiously, she clambered out of the back of the jeep.
She grabbed Jason's arm and gave him a restrained
kiss on the cheek, then scrambled into the passenger
seat. Jason looked at her suspiciously but Shannon,
having attained her objective, smiled at him con-
tentedly. She waved once and the car began to move
down the driveway.

Chapter 10

The plane from Aswan landed at the Cairo airport after a short and uneventful flight. In the bus that took them from the airport into the city, Cliff reviewed their schedule for the long day ahead.

"First of all, we'll have some breakfast. After that, we're free until eleven o'clock. That's when we met Ari. We'll have lunch with him and then get together with the minister at four. After that, we're free to do as we like until the bus takes us back to the airport in time for our eight o'clock flight."

They had planned to meet Ari for lunch at the Athor Hotel. Shannon smiled at her memories of the hotel. As she recalled, it was a pretty spot situated on the banks of the Nile, and a familiar one to her, since her grandfather had often stayed there when he went to Cairo on business.

As the bus pulled out of the airport and turned onto the main highway, Cliff and Shannon gazed with interest at the wide, open countryside that soon gave away to the heavily populated suburbs of the capital of Egypt, whose population exceeded five million. As they neared the great city, which stretched out along both banks of the Nile, they could see its outlines rising softly through the light morning mists, its graceful minarets and domed mosques standing high against the pale sky. It was a cosmopolitan city, alive, vital, housing people of many nationalities. People, trucks, buses, cars, bicycles, horse-drawn wagons and even the occasional herd of sheep crammed its teeming streets. The traffic was heavy and the streets noisy; the city's gates were guarded by soldiers of the national army. In the midst of the noise and apparent confusion, however, Shannon noticed several large, luxuriant gardens, island of peace and tranquillity.

Although the Hotel Athor was located in the center of Cairo, it was surrounded by a marvelous garden of soaring palms and gigantic banana trees with large, heavy leaves. Built twelve years ago, the hotel had escaped the latest garish trends in modern architecture and its soothing, clean, classical lines were pleasing in such lush surroundings. It was a welcome oasis in the busy hum of downtown Cairo, well known for its good food and excellent service.

Sitting out on the shaded terrace, Shannon and Cliff relaxed over a leisurely breakfast. The terrace was lovely, and as they enjoyed their meal, they luxuriated in the sweet scents of the highly perfumed flowers from the surrounding gardens and in the cool, morning air and fresh breezes that came from the nearby river. Waiters in native costume hovered noiselessly over their table, unobtrusively seeing to their every need. It was so peaceful and quiet that Shannon found it hard to believe she was in the middle of a busy metropolis. The noises from the city were muffled and dulled by the thick foliage of the trees and gardens around the terrace. In the east, the sun was slowly rising in the sky, piercing through the light morning mists. It was going to a beautiful, clear day.

As she finished her coffee, Shannon looked up and caught Cliff staring at her intently. When she met his eyes, a sudden warmth flooded through her body.

"How are we going to spend our free time here?" she asked awkwardly.

"I have nothing definite planned for the morning," Cliff replied, in answer to her question. "I remember you said you didn't know Cairo very well. I don't either, as a matter of fact—I've only seen what Ari has shown me. But it's a city that has always fascinated me. How about you?" he asked, smiling in response to Shannon's nods, her obvious, eager agreement. "Well," he went on, "if you haven't made other plans, we could explore the city together."

Shannon eagerly accepted. Before long they were both examining a map of the city Cliff had bought on his first visit to Egypt.

"We could start off by visiting the citadel and the Mokkatam," he said, as he pointed out various places on the map. "And then I'd like to just wander around and explore the tiny, out-of-the-way streets and shops. I wish we had more time, really. There's much to see. I could easily spend a week here."

A short time later, a taxi dropped them off in front

of the imposing doors of the citadel, which had been
built over eight hundred years before. With a sense of
shared awe, they entered the building, eventually
coming out onto the Mokkatam, a hill that dom-
inated the entire city. The view was magnificent.
They could see, stretching for miles before them, the
beautiful lands around the Nile and the modern
section of the city.

"Do you see that patch of green beside the high-rise
building over there?" Cliff asked, pointing beyond
the river. "That's the garden where we had breakfast
this morning."

Shannon shaded her eyes but couldn't locate the
spot he was pointing to. Cliff put his arm around her
shoulder to guide her in the right direction, his head
close to hers. "Over there," he said. "Next to that
tower."

Shannon strained to locate the patch of green he
was referring to, but her attention was drawn away
by her trembling awareness of his hand on her bare
shoulder and his head so close to hers.

"Do you see it?" he asked again, his voice
betraying a certain huskiness. His fingers lightly
caressed her skin and he turned to face her.

"No—no, I'm afraid I . . . ." But she couldn't say
any more.

"See the tower?"

"Oh, now I see it," she said with relief, the vision
of that simple square of green a moment of clarity in
a swirl of emotions. Her heart was pounding. She felt
him drawing her tenderly toward him. She longed to
be in his arms, to kiss him. The strength of her desire

was new and frightening, almost overwhelming. Abruptly, she pulled away and stood nervously out of his reach.

"Yes, that's the Hotel Athor all right," she replied hastily, nervously, trembling with frustrated desire.

Cliff drew himself away, but said nothing for the moment. When Shannon glanced at him briefly, she was struck by the severe look on his face, almost as if it had been carved out of marble.

"Well, let's be on our way," he said at last, taking her arm.

"Of course," Shannon said, with a sigh of relief and a feeling of sinking disappointment at the same time.

They took a cab to the Turkish bazaar and visited the booths of highly skilled craftsmen who worked in leather, wood and ivory. The air was dry, hot and laden with the heady aromas of spices. Caught up in the exotic atmosphere of the market, they lost all track of time as they wandered through the narrow streets lined with stalls selling wares of all descriptions.

At one point, they stopped at a jeweler's booth where Shannon picked out a gold necklace and held it to her neck in front of a little mirror provided for customers. "That really suits you," Cliff commented admiringly.

She glanced briefly in his direction, then replaced the necklace, a look of disappointment in her eyes. "It would really look much better on someone with a darker complexion than mine," she replied.

"Who, for example?" he asked.

"Divina."

"You seem to think of her a lot," he remarked quietly, as their eyes met and held. "Why is that?"

Even though she knew her answer might disrupt the feeling growing between them, she nevertheless decided to risk saying what was on her mind. "Ever since you and she arrived at the hospital, I've been trying to figure out what there is between you."

"How could there be anything between us . . . she won't even speak to me," Cliff said sadly. "And you're wrong, in any case, about that necklace," he added uncomfortably, obviously changing the subject. "Take another look."

He picked up the fragile gold chain from its purple velvet display case. There was a handsome pendant in the shape of a bird, its wings spread in a gesture of freedom and joy, dangling from the delicate golden thread. Finely inlaid precious and semi-precious stones represented the tiny feathers in the tips of the wings.

"It's really amazing," Shannon exclaimed, looking at the necklace more closely this time. "It must be worth a fortune."

Cliff carefully lifted the long, blond hair at the nape of her neck and slipped the necklace in place. "There," he said, his hands on her shoulders, looking at her reflection in the mirror. "You look so beautiful," he added simply. "I like you with your hair down like this."

Shannon smiled and looked away. She wasn't accustomed to receiving compliments. Nor was she accustomed to thinking of herself as beautiful. She looked at her reflection in the mirror. Her gray eyes looked clear, open and bright; her skin was translucent; her lips full and rosy with color. Light wisps of hair innocently framed her oval face. The graceful, simple lines of the necklace appealed to her. She liked the way the bird's wings opened so elegantly and so protectively in the slender hollow of her neck.

"It's a good luck symbol," the shopkeeper said in Arabic. "And an antique. Very valuable," he noted.

"How much?" Cliff asked, coming directly to the point.

"Cliff . . . I can't even consider it. Not under the circumstances. You know what our position is at the hospital and . . . ."

The shopkeeper mumbled a figure. There could be no doubt about the value of the necklace. The merchant was asking for more than one thousand American dollars.

"The gold and gems alone are worth more," the shopkeeper noted persuasively.

"I'm afraid it's out of the question," Shannon said sadly but firmly, slipping the necklace off and returning it to its case. She tugged on Cliff's arm. "Come on," she said playfully. "It's dangerous around here. We'd better scat!"

"But . . . ."

"No, Cliff. I want to go," she said.

They turned away and continued through the market. Before long, the intoxicating smells and and sounds overcame them and the necklace became only one of many irresistible impressions. They laughed, they joked, they explored . . . they reveled in the excitement of this dense world packed with vendors, shoppers, animals and crafts.

A little before eleven o'clock they headed back to the hotel. They were tired and excited, and Shannon had barely enough time to freshen up for their luncheon appointment with Ari. In the pleasure of exploring the city with Cliff, she had almost forgotten the serious business of their visit. But now, thinking of it in the privacy of a quiet room, her stomach was in knots. What if these interviews did not go well? The hospital would collapse. They wouldn't be able to stay open. The responsibility was an awesome one, and there were many times when Shannon yearned to walk away from it, to be able to relax and enjoy life as those around her seemed to do.

Shannon smiled at the memory of the morning. It had been so refreshing to laugh and get caught up in a childlike sense of discovery. She splashed water on her cheeks and noticed again how clear and bright her eyes looked, how glowing her cheeks. *If everything goes well*, she thought, *I'm going to celebrate*.

When she walked into the lobby, she noticed Cliff standing by the window, tall and relaxed. He was certainly an attractive man, she thought. But most of all she liked how it felt to be with him.

"Hello . . . admiring the view?" she asked in a soft voice.

"Oh, yes," he said, turning to look at her with a tender smile. "I was just thinking how easy it would be to get addicted to this country. I have to admit it's getting under my skin."

"I know what you mean. I've been a desert addict for almost ten years now. I can't imagine any other way of life, actually. Sometime I'd like to show you the desert. Today we saw the crowds and it was easy to forget that not far away there is . . . nothing, as far as you can see. A place where it's always quiet, always empty. It's beautiful, I can't explain it."

Cliff looked intently at Shannon. He had never seen this side of her before.

"I'd like that," he said. "And that's why we've got to make this trip work," he said firmly, as if to himself.

A few moments later, Ari Khalam walked into the lobby. He was a slim, athletic looking man who wore his clothes with casual elegance. Above his dark brown eyes there was a mass of dark, curly hair and, when he smiled, his teeth were a brilliant white in contrast to his smooth, dark complexion. He shook Cliff's hand enthusiastically, obviously delighted to see his old friend again.

"I'm very happy to meet you, Dr. Mallison," he said, bowing slightly. "Cliff has told me all about you and the wonderful work you do at your hospital in Aswan. I wanted you to be my guests for lunch. However, Cliff insisted I come here instead. I submitted to his request—but I insist that you come back to my home later for some Turkish coffee," he added graciously.

On that note, they made their way to the dining room and were soon seated at the table Cliff had reserved.

Before long, the two men were reminiscing about

their university days but, as if by some secret agreement, they made no mention of Cliff's private life between the time when they had gone their separate ways in Paris so many years ago and when they'd met again in Cairo.

Eventually, the conversation turned to the Foundation and the purpose of Shannon's visit.

"I gave my uncle all the details Cliff sent me about the Mallison Hospital," Ari began. "He's been Minister of Health for just under a year now, and he said quite frankly that he didn't know very much about the Foundation at all. For the past few days, he's been studying all the related material he can get his hands on. He'll be delighted to meet with you this afternoon." Ari paused, smiling at Shannon's nervous grin. "I hope the interview goes well for you. Of course, I can't promise anything. My uncle's voice is a strong one, but it is only one of several."

Shannon thanked him gratefully for his help, and explained in more detail the financial difficulties of the Foundation. "This is our last chance," she said sadly. "If we don't convince the government how much we need that subsidy, we won't be in business too much longer."

"I believe my uncle realizes that," Ari assured her. "So, please, don't give up hope yet."

The conversation at lunch was warm, lively and interesting. When the meal was over, Cliff and Shannon accepted Ari's invitation to have coffee at his home.

The young surgeon was a bachelor and lived in a beautiful apartment in the new section of the city. In the cool, relaxed atmosphere of his home, Cliff and Shannon spent a pleasant half hour chatting with their host and enjoying the rich, dark Turkish coffee. As the time for the interview drew near, Ari offered to drop them off at his uncle's office, which was on the way to the hospital where he had his practice. When they reached the office of the Minister of Health, they said goodbye, promising to phone Ari from Aswan the next day to tell him how the interview went.

The minister didn't keep them waiting and they were shown immediately into his office. He was a pleasant looking man in his mid-fifties who spoke English fluently. He seemed honored to meet Cliff; he had read in the newspapers of his pioneering work in transplant surgery in Europe.

After a few pleasantries, he asked his two visitors about their problem. He sat quietly while Shannon presented her case. She spoke passionately about her grandfather's work, and described how she was trying to carry on in his footsteps with the help of a few dedicated colleagues. Then Cliff went into a long, detailed analysis of the Foundation and its contribution to the community at large.

After listening carefully to Cliff's clean exposition, the minister read the governor's letter, taking note of the influential signatures, and then read through the report. After asking a series of questions designed to give him a clear picture of the hospital's financial difficulties, he asked each of them to tell him something about their own area of competence. After a moment's silence, which to Shannon seemed like an eternity, he said, "I've asked my staff to provide some details for me and to do some research. There can be no doubt—the work your hospital has done to fight schistosomiasis has been admirable. And all the general hospital care you provide, especially in obstetrics, is of the highest order—it's even bringing international recognition to our country. All this is excellent. Therefore it is with some embarrassment that I must ask you to explain an incident that has appeared in our confidential reports . . . ."

Shannon looked at Cliff, trying not to appear alarmed.

" . . . and that has to do with some mysterious missing quantities of amyl nitrate a short time ago. From what my reports said, there was some suspicion that you, Dr. Mallison, might have been responsible—that the requisition forms were in your name. Have you anything to say to that charge, Dr. Mallison?"

"Yes, I do. We checked all our records in an attempt to understand that incident. The forms were in my name, but not in my handwriting. So far as we were able to determine, all the orders were passed through the drug-supply department at a time when there was a relatively young, inexperienced attendant on staff, someone who wasn't familiar with our procedures. It so happened that we never did find out who was behind the incident. We have solved the problem, we believe, by requiring two signatures on every request, one of which must be mine, and by making sure that there are always two attendants in the drug-supply room at all times. So far, we have not had a recurrence of the problem. As you might imagine, we are watching the situation very closely."

Shannon was nervous, but her nervousness didn't show. She spoke confidently and with conviction. Cliff gazed at her with pride.

The minister watched her carefully. He was accustomed to evaluating people for telltale signs of the emotions that would show when a person was lying. He couldn't afford to recommend giving funds to the Mallison Foundation, and then to have it discovered that the hospital was a thriving, black-market drug outlet. He knew how such mistakes would look on his record.

He believed her. There was no reason he should, really. It was her word against the rumors that were floating around, rumors he had often enough found cause to believe. This time, however, he knew the rumors were untrue. He would be willing to bet his life on it—more practically, he was willing to bet his job.

"Very well," he said simply. "I believe you. How do they say it in your native country? Case dismissed?"

Shannon and Cliff smiled and nodded.

"Yes? Well, then, case dismissed. I will take the matter under serious consideration and promise to do everything in my power to convince the commission that you deserve the money you request." He paused for a moment, glancing at his two visitors. "It seems to me that the Mallison Foundation must be recognized for all the good work it's doing for the community. It needs outside help in order to continue, and it should get that help. So I intend to present your report personally to the chairman of the commission. Although I can't promise you anything, I can say I feel optimistic about the success of your mission here. For the moment, however, I can only encourage you to keep up the good work, and I thank you and your colleagues for the service you've been providing for the people of Aswan all these years. I'll keep you informed, and I'll call you as soon as I know the commission's decision."

When they left the minister's office and walked out into the busy city streets, the sun was setting slowly over the Nile.

"Do you think he was really impressed with our presentation?" Shannon asked anxiously. "Do you think we have a chance?"

"I'm sure of it. We have a very powerful ally in the minister," Cliff assured her. "Also, as Dr. Mallison's granddaughter and as a doctor yourself, you really impressed him, to say nothing of how enchanting he found you as a woman."

Shannon smiled happily, her eyes brilliant with pleasure at his gracious compliment.

"It wasn't all me, Cliff," she replied gently. "You contributed a great deal. He was certainly pleased to meet you. I just want to tell you how grateful I am to you for all your help. If it weren't for you, I wouldn't have had this interview. You made it all possible."

"It's Ari you should be thanking, not me."

"It's you," she said stubbornly. "I don't know how I can ever thank you."

"You've already done that," he replied gravely.

"What do you mean?"

"By giving me the chance to work at the Foundation."

Suddenly, the rush of words and questions held back for so long sprang to her lips, but she was unable to speak. For a minute, Shannon thought he was going to talk to her about his past, but he tensed almost immediately and looked quickly at his watch.

"We have over an hour before we have to be at the airport," he remarked. "Would you like to go back to that little patch of green by the Nile?"

Feeling slightly disappointed, she nodded quickly as they started walking slowly back in the direction of the Athor Hotel. They crossed El Tahrir bridge and strolled through the lush Andalusian Gardens on Gezira Island, enjoying the cool green shade that was a welcome refuge from the heat of the late-afternoon sun.

As Cliff helped her up the steps of a small stone bridge, he took her hand in his and didn't let go. Shannon's emotions were in a turmoil. She felt deeply troubled by his touch, but she could not bring herself to take her hand from his gentle grasp.

They walked on like that together in silence, Shannon only aware of that tiny part of her body where their skin lightly touched.

I can't let this happen, she thought.

But before she had a chance to protest, Cliff took her in his arms and held her, pressing her hungrily against him. His mouth searched for hers and he kissed her deeply, moaning with pleasure to feel her response, her total, trembling answer to his touch.

As his lips enveloped hers, the whole world seemed to tilt, and they abandoned themselves to the power of their feelings for each other.

When he let her go, she turned away from him, shaken and breathless, suddenly overcome with guilt. *What am I doing,* she thought frantically. *What about Jason? How can I be doing this to him?*

What excuses did she have for giving in to Cliff's kisses, for allowing herself to be deeply stirred by him when she was engaged to Jason? Suddenly, she realized that nothing was simple in life, that clinging firmly to one's principles really didn't solve every problem that came up, and that human nature was weak and flawed. In that one moment of insight, as she examined her own behavior, she began to understand her stepsister for the first time.

"Are you okay?" Cliff asked, his voice thick with emotion. He noticed how pale she had become, and how tense she looked. "Are you angry?"

"No, of course not," she replied, shaking her head slowly, not daring to look at him. "I'm to blame."

Feeling at a complete loss, she tried desperately to find the words that would explain how she felt and prevent this kind of thing from happening again.

Cliff took her by the shoulders and turned her to face him. "Why are you so torn? I thought . . . I thought you cared for me . . . that you wanted . . . but you don't. You really *aren't* free, are you?"

Shannon shook her head. "I'm engaged to Jason—and I've promised I'll marry him."

"Do you always keep your promises?"

"Yes, I do. Especially to Jason. We get along well together, and he's . . . he's very helpful."

"Do you love him?"

"I'm sorry. I don't feel I should have to say any more than I have. I'm finding this very upsetting. I've said too much already."

Cliff placed his hands on his hips, and stood looking out over the river. "There was so much that I . . ." he began, and then stopped abruptly. Shannon realized that he was as upset as she was. She longed to go to him and comfort him, but she kept herself in check.

"I want you to know something, then I'll never say another word, I promise you," he said deliberately, weighing each word. "You have given me something, something that means a great deal to me. When we first met, I told you I knew what it was like to break down and cry. I knew a woman once—many, many years ago—and she died. She died in my arms in a car accident. I haven't cared for a woman since. Oh, there have been many casual friends, but my heart was never touched. I thought it had died with her. You've made me feel things I thought I would never feel again, and for this I will always be grateful to you. I . . . I love you, Shannon. I think I've always loved you. I've never met a woman quite like you."

"Please, stop. Don't say any more," she pleaded.

"You're right. I won't say anything more. But I have one small thing to ask of you."

Shannon looked at him unhappily. She was feeling so many different, strong emotions that she felt like she was being torn apart inside.

"Don't look so miserable!" Cliff said with a laugh, forcing Shannon to laugh along with him. "I know it must be painful, being told how lovely you are . . . ."

"Cliff! You promised!" she exclaimed, hitting him playfully on the shoulder, tears of joy and pain streaming down her cheeks.

"Peace! Peace and love," he chanted in mock surrender. "Seriously," he added, straightening up, "I want you to take something . . . . But only on the condition that we never, ever speak about it again. This is important to me . . . I insist."

Shannon found his request a curious one, but he was so adamant and she was so eager to please that she agreed. As they turned to walk back into the city to catch a bus to the airport, he slipped a small parcel into her pocket. "And you can't open it until midnight. Promise, friend?" he asked, extending his hand.

"I promise," she said, smiling through her tears and taking his hand.

Chapter 11

Shannon boarded the bus with relief. After the scene with Cliff, she was glad of the presence of other people. She needed to collect her thoughts. In a few hours, she would be back in Aswan. Back with Jason and the Foundation . . . back where she belonged. She would be on home ground; the spell of this interlude with Cliff would be broken and, with coming of a new day, things would return to normal.

When they arrived at the airport, they had to wait almost an hour before their plane took off.

"I promised Jason I would call him," she said quietly. "Would you excuse me for a moment?" she added, smiling at Cliff.

As she headed for the phone booth in the airport lobby, there was an announcement over the loudspeaker. The flight to Aswan had been cancelled because of high winds that had been sweeping across the upper Nile region for a few hours. Atmospheric conditions were very bad and the announcement said, flying was impossible.

"What are we going to do?" Shannon asked, turning to Cliff in panic.

"I don't know. Does this sort of thing happen often?"

"I don't know . . . . I don't leave the Foundation often."

"There must be a train for Aswan this evening. Cliff went to the counter to check. A few moments later he was back. "There is," he said, "but it's already left. And besides, we wouldn't get to Aswan until tomorrow morning—the train takes twelve hours. We'll just have to spend the night in Cairo."

"I guess so," Shannon replied, upset at this unexpected turn of events.

"Do you want me to call Ari and ask him to put us up for the night? I'm sure he would be glad to have us."

"I don't want to impose on him any further, Cliff. I think I'd rather stay in a hotel."

Cliff agreed this was the best thing to do under the circumstances and, after finding out what time the first plane left in the morning, they boarded a bus that took them back to the Athor Hotel.

When they walked into the lobby, Cliff went straight to the reception desk and asked if there were still rooms available for that evening. The receptionist looked up at him, smiled and announced that there was one lovely one left that had a private bath and a magnificent view of the Nile. Neither Shannon nor Cliff smiled at the clerk's mistaken assumption. "We want two separate rooms," Cliff explained brusquely.

"Oh, excuse me. In that case, we have two small adjoining rooms on the second floor."

"Is that all?" Cliff asked crisply.

"I'm afraid so."

"We'll have to take them, then."

BEFORE JOINING CLIFF in the hotel dining room, Shannon took note of the communicating door between their two rooms and quietly locked it.

When she walked into the lobby, Cliff was waiting for her and led her to their table. They enjoyed a leisurely meal but the conversation was stilted, each one acutely aware of the emotional interlude in the gardens on Gezira Island.

"Let's go and visit Gizeh," Cliff suggested, as the meal drew to a close. "I've heard that the pyramids are fantastic at night. It's only nine o'clock. We can't call it a night this early," he added, noting her reluctance. "There are so many wonderful things to see—we might as well take advantage of the time we have and see as much as we can while we're here. And I promise I'll be a perfect gentleman."

Shannon laughed and graciously relented. Before long they were in a cab heading for the Mena House Hotel.

Refusing the usual guides with their endless chatter, they paid the admission price and set out to see the pyramids themselves.

They peered uncertainly into the black night. Then, out of the darkness, the great structures loomed up before them, illuminated by giant spotlights. Their colossal splendor rose majestically against the deep blue of the night sky. Nearby, a cluster of shops selling necklaces, souvenirs and little plaster models of the pyramids did a thriving business. Even this blatant commercialism couldn't shatter the awesome spell of the sacred structures.

Awed by the ancient grandeur, Shannon and Cliff walked silently toward the tombs of the pharaohs. Standing in the timeless desert, the monuments were silent witnesses to the birth and death of civilizations now buried at their feet.

"How can we take our problems seriously?" Shannon said softly. "When I look at these, I feel so small. It's a good feeling, in a way, you know. I like knowing I'm part of something this timeless."

They lingered near the Cheops pyramid for a while, then moved on to the Sphinx, that monumental stone lion with a human head, sadly disfigured by the onslaught of invading Mamluks centuries earlier.

"The mystery of life and death is etched on her face," Cliff murmured pensively, feeling the impact of the ancient stone structures.

Shannon shivered in the cool night air and thought longingly of her warm hotel room. At that moment, she wanted nothing more than to go back to her room and take refuge in the glorious oblivion of sleep, where she could forget all about the universe and the pain and difficulty of life.

"Let's go back, Cliff," she said suddenly.

Cliff found a young boy who wanted to earn a couple of pennies and asked him to get them a taxi. In no time, an old cab pulled up in front of them. Without a word, they got in and returned to their hotel.

When they saw the name of their hotel shining out

among the other neon signs on Alexandria Boulevard, Cliff laughed and said, "Athor, Goddess of love and desire, will watch over us tonight."

They said good-night formally to each other when they reached their rooms and went their separate ways, not daring to shake hands.

As Shannon was undressing, she found the small parcel in her pocket. She had almost forgotten about the strange pact she and Cliff had so formally agreed on. She glanced at the clock; it was still fifteen minutes before midnight. She had promised she wouldn't open her gift until the witching hour, so she made her bed ready and snuggled in, luxuriating in the crisp comfort of fresh sheets. She noticed the light shining under the door that led to Cliff's room. For a while, she heard him pacing up and down. She couldn't help wondering what was going through his mind.

Slowly the hands on the clock moved to point to midnight. She opened the tiny parcel and gasped when she saw what was inside: it was the gold necklace. Tears came to her eyes. *Oh, Cliff,* she thought, *how could you do such a thing?* She had to make him return it—it was such an outrageous luxury. She could see why he had made her promise not to open it until now. And she had also promised never to speak to him about it. She knew it wouldn't be easy to keep that second promise—but she'd have to try.

She examined the necklace closely, admiring the intricate detail of the jeweled bird. It was more and more beautiful each time she saw it. She slipped it around her neck and looked in the mirror. *This necklace is going to turn me into a vain woman,* she thought with a chuckle. *I can't stop admiring myself when I'm wearing it!*

Perhaps the hardest part of their bargain was that she was unable even to express her thanks or her joy. Cliff's light was still on. No doubt he was listening for her reaction to the midnight present. She went to the adjoining door and made what she hoped would be a joyful-sounding tap. Then she went to bed, her necklace under her pillow for good luck.

AT LUNCHTIME CAROL found herself alone, as usual. At one of the nearby tables, Jason and Bechir were involved in a lively discussion. They were just finishing their coffee when a nurse came in asking for Dr. Hinawi.

As Bechir got up to leave, Jason glanced quickly at Carol, then walked over to her table. "You've hardly eaten anything," he observed. "Aren't you feeling well?"

"I'm fine," she replied dully.

"You don't look it. You haven't been yourself for a long time now, ever since your . . . What should I call it? Your accident?"

"You can call it whatever you want," she replied, blushing furiously.

Jason's eyes seemed to pierce right through her and she lowered her own eyes. Wordlessly, she began fiddling with a piece of pastry, which up until then had lain on her plate untouched.

"I think I should check you over and take a blood sample. Come and see me this afternoon in my office."

"I don't think that's necessary, Jason. I'm feeling fine, really."

"Just the same, I want to see you. I'll expect you around three o'clock," he replied imperiously.

With a sudden and complete switch of mood, Carol docilely agreed to appear.

The examination room was clean and tidy, furnished with only the bare essentials: a desk, two chairs, a small cupboard and a medicine cabinet.

"Sit down," Jason said, greeting her. "You'll have to forgive me—I'm a little confused today. It started out with a strange phone call just as I was going to the airport. Someone told me a patient of mine was sick. Well, you can imagine how I felt when I found no trace of anything—no phone call, no patient. You wouldn't know anything about that would you?" he added, an edge of sarcasm in his voice.

"Of course not."

"Well, okay. Forget it. First of all, I'm going to take a blood sample so the lab people can start working on it right away."

When he had taken a small amount of blood and sent it down to the lab, he turned back to Carol and looked at her closely. "How is your leg? Has there been any more swelling?"

"No, it's fine."

"Let me see."

She pulled up her skirt and he examined the inside of her thigh carefully. It was just as she said. The leg was completely healed and the swelling had disappeared. Only a little scratch remained, where the scorpion's stinger had pierced the skin.

He looked at it more closely, examining the little

bump with his fingers. "The muscles are still a bit flaccid," he commented factually, looking up at her with a blank expression on his face. "But aside from that, I think the leg is doing just fine."

"I—I told you it was okay," Carol stammered, as she quickly pulled down her skirt.

"I'm more concerned about your emotional health," Jason said, throwing her an inquisitive glance. "You haven't been yourself for quite some time now. Are you sleeping well?"

"Very well."

"No bouts of depression?"

"Why should I be depressed?" she asked, shrugging her shoulders indifferently.

"You know the answer to that better than I do. Tell me the truth," he insisted, knowing she was trying to avoid his questions. "You're not in good shape, either physically or emotionally. Now, why don't you tell me what's wrong? You're not on any drugs, are you?"

"Nothing out of the ordinary," she answered sullenly. "Let's just say I feel more exhausted and depressed than usual. It's nothing serious."

"I'm worried about this lethargy and your overall lack of energy," he said, sitting down behind his desk. "I'm going to prescribe something for you, but I think the real cure lies with you. You've got to get out more, have some fun. You've been alone too much lately."

She didn't say a word as he wrote up a prescription and handed it to her. "Take this to Stella Drake— she'll fill it for you. Now, promise me you'll get out and get some exercise. As a matter of fact, I'm playing tennis with Bechir tonight. Would you like to join us?"

Carol declined his invitation and quietly left the office, her cheeks flushed. She couldn't decide if Jason's invitation had been sincere, or if he had been making fun of her. Toward the late afternoon, Carol suddenly ran to the phone and called Jason on the intercom system that connected the staff houses.

"Is your offer for tennis still open for tonight?" she asked as soon as she heard his voice.

"Why? Have you changed your mind?"

"Yes, I have."

"It's getting pretty cloudy and there's a bit of a wind, but I think we'll have time for a game or two. I'll meet you out on the courts in ten minutes. Okay?"

"Great," she said, her voice betraying her excitement.

When she reached the courts, Dr. Hinawi was not there. Jason explained that one of his patients had gone into labor and he had had to stay at the hospital.

It was getting very windy. They only had time for one game, which Carol lost. She played very badly: she was completely out of shape and, after a few minutes, was totally exhausted. She looked weak, worn out, drained of all energy.

Jason noticed her condition immediately and walked over to her. "That's enough for today. You don't want to tire yourself your first time out. Besides, it looks like we're in for a bad storm. We should get inside right away."

Carol was looking very pale and beads of perspiration had broken out on her forehead. She nodded quietly and slipped into her sweater.

"Come on back to my place," Jason suggested. "Bechir should be back soon and we can all have a drink together."

When they reached Jason's house, Dr. Hinawi had not yet returned. The wind had risen fast. It howled around the house; the air was full of dust, the trees bent almost double by the force of the gale. One of the shutters was flapping wildly and Jason went over to fasten it more securely. When he had closed the window and handed Carol a gin and tonic, she asked him when Shannon and Cliff were expected back.

"Around ten o'clock, I think. That is, if the flight isn't cancelled because of this storm."

"Are you going to meet them at the airport?"

"No, I don't think so," he replied, remembering that Shannon had asked him to wait for her at home. "Yassef will go. I promised Bechir I would be around the house this evening."

His words were cut short by the phone ringing. "Excuse me," he said, walking quickly to the phone in the hallway.

He had been waiting for this call impatiently all day, and he picked up the receiver with great anticipation, smiling when he heard Shannon's voice on the other end of the line. He listened carefully as she told him about her interview with the Minister of Health and promised to tell him about it in more detail when she got back. Then she told him her flight had been cancelled and that she and Cliff wouldn't be back until the next day.

"We're having a very bad storm here ourselves,"

Jason replied calmly. "I thought your plane might be grounded. Where will you be spending the night?"

"At the Hotel Athor. I'm calling from there right now. It's annoying being stuck here like this—I wanted to get right back home. I want to see you. But I'm afraid there's nothing I can do."

Despite her strong feelings for Cliff, Shannon meant what she said. After the short but powerful interlude in the Andalusian Gardens, and her guilt reaction afterward, all she wanted to do was run into Jason's arms and take refuge in his reassuring presence. She was afraid to be alone with Cliff any more. She was as frightened of her own feelings as she was of his, and longed to be back in the familiar safety and security of the hospital.

"I know Carol won't really care whether I'm delayed or not," she continued. "But would you tell her I won't be back tonight anyway? Divina should be told, too. And, Jason, could you ask her not to prepare any patients for the operations that were scheduled for tomorrow?"

Jason agreed to pass on the messages. After a few parting words, Shannon said goodbye and hung up.

When Jason returned to the living room, Carol was leafing casually through a magazine. "So, what's the news from Cairo?"

"Well, it seems the interview went very well. However, Cliff and Shannon won't be back until tomorrow. Their flight was cancelled because of the storm. Shannon asked me to tell you she wouldn't be home tonight," he replied, as he sat on the couch beside her.

"Why didn't they take the train?" Carol asked, looking at him.

"There's only one and they probably missed it—it likely left before their flight was cancelled."

Carol watched him silently. She looked up at him, feigning innocence, and said, "They had a long evening ahead of them. What do you think they're going to do?"

Jason shrugged his shoulders indifferently. "There's a lot to do in Cairo. I don't think they'll get bored."

"I don't, either," Carol murmured knowingly.

Jason looked at her in silence for a moment, a strange expression in his eyes. Then he suddenly grabbed her by the waist and forced her down onto the couch.

"No!" Carol said. "Stop. Let me go!" She struggled vainly against him, panting with effort, flailing her arms helplessly as she felt his hand familiarly stroking her thigh.

"Please!" she cried out, a mingled gasp of both pleasure and pain.

"You know you want this as much as I do," Jason growled, then he pinned her arms to the sofa above her head and stretched his body on top of hers. But his eyes never left her face, and they gleamed strangely. "You little minx . . . you've known I wanted you. But I couldn't afford to upset all my plans."

"What do you mean, plans?" Carol gasped.

"Do you think I've been staying in this backwater, sweating my guts out, because I'm a great humanitarian? I've stayed and pretended to be in love with Shannon so I could marry her and get control of the hospital. Then, eventually, my name would become world famous. And I'd have a beautiful wife; Shannon isn't bad to look at—but she's cold. Not like you, baby. Not like you at all." He lowered his head to hers and Carol tried to struggle once more. But her resistance was weakening.

"I nearly blew it all that night of the party," he panted hoarsely. "Every time I kissed Shannon I wanted you. And you stood there and watched. We're two of a kind, baby, you and me."

Slowly, Jason began to kiss her neck, working his way down her torso. But the abrupt sound of the front door opening brought him to his feet in a flash.

He ran his fingers through his hair and smoothed his clothing.

"It's Bechir," he said, going toward the door. "You're leaving."

Dr. Hinawi entered quickly. "The weather's terrible!" he exclaimed, unaware of the strained atmosphere in the living room, "You should see it out there."

Carol stood up and got ready to leave. "Well, I think I *will* see it. Good night, Bechir, Jason. And thanks for the game. You were right. It was an invigorating evening."

Jason made no effort to stop her and, when the door closed, he collapsed into a chair opposite Bechir, who was already starting to relax after a rough day.

Chapter 12

Cliff was just starting his rounds when Farah, one of the nurse's aides, ran up to him in the hall.

"Doctor, come quick, please," she cried. "It's Ella. She's fainted. I think she's really sick. Come quick, please."

A few minutes later, Cliff had the woman in his consulting room and was examining her thoroughly. When he had finished, there was an apprehensive expression in his dark eyes and he was frowning.

Ella lay on the bed, her face ashen, her body racked with fever. She was still unconscious and Cliff sent out a call for Shannon and Bechir to assist him immediately. This sudden attack of illness and fever, plus her symptoms, was alarming. He gave her a shot of antibiotics, then sent for one of the nurses to sit with the sick woman. Then, as soon as she was resting quietly with the nurse by her side, he left the room in search of Farah to ask her what had happened.

He found the young nurse's aide standing out in

the hall with Shannon. The girl was obviously still very upset and could hardly talk in a coherent fashion.

"We were just cleaning up the medical supply room when all of a sudden she said she had a bad headache. Then she fainted. I ran as fast as I could to get you."

"Go to Dr. Wilfred's house right away and tell him to meet me here immediately," Cliff said quietly.

As Farah hurried off down the hall, Shannon turned and looked at Cliff, a worried expression in her clear, gray eyes. "What's the matter, Cliff? Surely, it's not serious enough to warrant a consultation with three other doctors."

"I think it might be, Shannon. I haven't had a chance to tell you this but Ella is the second person in two days to get sick in exactly this way. Last night, one of Wilfred's patients who was scheduled for an operation today came down suddenly with the same symptoms."

Shannon suddenly felt worried. "Do you think there's a connection between the two cases? Maybe an epidemic of some kind?" she asked anxiously.

"I don't know. I've never seen anything like it," he said, trying to keep his voice calm. "But there's no point in worrying until we know more. Why don't you go back to your office and forget about this for a while? When Bechir and Jason show up, I'll contact you."

Realizing she wasn't doing anyone any good standing around in the hall on the edge of panic, Shannon turned and walked away.

Cliff opened the door to the sickroom and went straight over to the woman lying motionless on the bed. He had a suspicion about this strange illness, but he hoped he was wrong. *It can't be*, he thought. *It just can't be.*

AFTER A LENGTHY CONSULTATION, the four doctors identified the illness—and the picture was not a pretty one.

"Shannon, you must tell the rest of the staff immediately," Cliff anounced calmly, "and take all the necessary precautions. Get them all together right away for an emergency meeting."

Shannon felt weak. She looked at the three men, amazed at their apparent calm. She was feeling far from calm herself—her worst fears had become a reality. It was an epidemic all right, and of the worst possible kind. How could she tell a staff of friends, colleagues and family that they were living with death, and that . . . .

As Shannon stood lost in thought, Carol wandered into the room. She was wearing a transparent cotton caftan shirt, loosely covering tight black jeans.

"Where are you going?" Shannon asked, taking in her stepsister's provocative attire.

"To the local hot spot, the cafeteria." Carol laughed throatily. "Where else *is* there?"

"Well, I'm glad you wandered in—I was just going to see you," Shannon said. "Until further notice, you won't be able to leave the hospital grounds—nobody will. There's been an emergency."

"What?" Carol asked in utter amazement.

"We have two cases of a very contagious disease on our hands. A man who was bitten by a rat very recently and a young nurse's aide. Certain precautions have to go into effect immediately, and the quarantine is one of them. We're having a staff meeting right away to discuss what measures to take. I expect you to be there, too, Carol."

"What's the disease?" she asked, frowning deeply.

"We haven't been able to give it a name, nor have the international specialists we've been consulting with. But one thing is clear—it's very similar to another, ancient disease. It may, in fact, be a modern variation. . . ."

"And what is that?"

"Well, I won't bother you with the scientific name. It wouldn't mean anything to you, anyway."

"Just tell me, will you! Stop hedging. . . ."

"It's the bubonic plague."

Shannon's words fell like a bomb in the silence of the room. Carol stood there gazing at the four doctors in horror.

"Are you sure?" Carol asked incredulously, looking from one face to another, her voice shaking with fear.

"Yes, Carol, I'm afraid so," Cliff broke in. "Shannon, Jason, Bechir and I are all in agreement. We've checked and double-checked in the lab, and there's no doubt about it. We've identified and isolated the bacteria. It's the plague, all right."

"But . . . but it doesn't seem possible," Carol said, trying to curb the panic rising in her throat.

"I interrogated the patients who shared the room

with the first man who got sick. He was one of Wilfred's patients. They told me he came into the hospital for an operation. . . ."

Carol stood shaking, utterly speechless, her face white and drawn. Cliff realized how she was feeling and tried to calm the young woman down. "You must help us, Carol. While the staff is gathering for the meeting, I want you to go get Yassef. I want you to explain the situation to him. He has to shut the main gates and prevent anyone from entering or leaving the hospital grounds."

Losing control of herself completely, Carol shook her head violently and began screaming. "Don't drag me into this, do you hear? Do you think I'm going to stay here and get infected, too? Are you crazy? I'm not part of the medical staff around here. You have no right to keep me here."

Jason grabbed her by the shoulders and began shaking her. "Carol! Shut up and pull yourself together," he said through clenched teeth. "Keep your voice down. The last thing we need around here is panic."

"I won't shut up. No one is going to stop me from leaving. Take your hands off me! Let me go!" she screamed.

Realizing she was almost out of control and fast becoming hysterical, Jason rushed across the room, picked up a carafe of water and threw it over her.

Gasping for air and more surprised than insulted, Carol suddenly burst into convulsive sobs.

"You . . . you dirty old man!" she hissed through

her tears. "You rapist! That's all you are. If you touch me again, I'll. . . ."

But for the sound of Carol's sobs, the room was silent.

"I'm sorry," Jason murmured contritely.

Shannon was distressed by her stepsister's reaction. Was Carol going crazy? She had always been quick to fly off the handle, but her reaction today was far worse than usual. Shannon walked slowly over to her stepsister and gently pushed back the strands of wet hair clinging to her strained features.

"Please, try to calm down, Carol," she said softly. "If you don't want to come to the staff meeting, you don't have to. Go on back to the house and try to relax."

Carol sniffed back her tears and left the room without another word.

"Well," Shannon sighed when the door closed behind Carol. She glanced at the other doctors. Jason's face was blotched and red. "I don't know what to say," she added.

"Well . . . on the positive side, we have some idea of the emotions we will be running up against," Cliff commented soberly. "Everyone values his life—we all do—and to be forced to . . . to tangle with death on such a minute-by-minute basis—it isn't going to be easy," he added huskily, his blue eyes looking directly at Shannon.

Shannon's heart jumped. Ever since the trip to Cairo the week before it had become more and more difficult for her to deny the strength of her feelings for Cliff. Sometimes when she was near him she felt she was in the grip of a powerful tidal wave over which she had no control. Her emotions made her increasingly uneasy, and she sought shelter blindly in the security of Jason's arms.

What had Carol meant by her words? Although she often said outrageous things, Shannon had never known her to lie. And Carol had called Jason a rapist! The very thought made Shannon laugh. In all the time that they had known each other, Jason had never so much as pressured her. He had been extremely patient about her lack of responsiveness, and for this Shannon had always been grateful.

Shannon glanced toward Jason, but he seemed too preoccupied to notice. Had Carol's remarks upset him, she wondered.

"The medical situation is the priority," Cliff was saying, "but I think we must all realize that if emotional panic sets in, all is lost. We must maintain control. And I think that control begins and ends with us—the four of us here. If we can set an example, show the others there is reason to think positively, then I think maybe, just maybe, we *will* be able to make it through." Cliff had stood up and was pacing around the room while he was talking. He stopped in front of the window and gazed out thoughtfully. It reminded Shannon of the way he had stood by the window in Cairo, at the hotel.

Shannon glanced at Bechir and Jason once again. Jason looked pale, and Shannon wondered if he were even listening. He seemed preoccupied with thoughts of his own. Bechir was clearly quite upset, but

Shannon noticed that Cliff's words had a calming effect upon him. Cliff certainly knew how to express something in a way that made sense, Shannon thought admiringly. He seemed to be able to make people feel that a sordid tragedy was merely an opportunity for heroism; he was inspiring. He made her feel that she did have the strength to face anything, and that together . . . .

"What can we do to stop the disease from spreading?" Shannon asked abruptly.

"We'll have to notify the authorities at the public hospital right away," Cliff answered. "And then we must find the family of the man who carried the infection in here in the first place and get them vaccinated immediately. Their house will have to be disinfected, as well . . . .

"I think I should call Ari in Cairo and ask him to tell the Committee of Health and Welfare what's happened here. They'll have to send us all the vaccine and streptomycin they can get their hands on. How much do we have on hand?"

Shannon opened the book where she kept track of all the medical supplies. After a rapid examination of the contents, she announced, "We have enough serum to start injections right away, and hopefully more will arrive from Cairo before we run out. We have some streptomycin, but not much. We'll just have to go with the vaccine until more drugs get here."

"All right, that should get us going. We'll have to isolate the two plague cases and inoculate the entire staff as well as all other patients in the hospital.

We've got to cancel all visits and prevent anyone from going home. It's going to be a big job and we're going to have our hands full. If we move fast, and don't lose our heads, I think we can cope with it." He paused, looking at his three listeners intently.

"To eliminate all risk of contagion, no one will be allowed to enter or leave the Foundation. We'll be under a very strict quarantine. But, at all costs, we must avoid panic. We'll meet with the rest of the hospital staff as soon as we can, explain the situation to them and insist on total cooperation. And Shannon, you and Bechir must isolate the maternity ward completely."

Shannon was again impressed with the new surgeon. Cliff was a man of action in times of crisis and could make quick, clear-cut decisions. As he outlined the emergency measures that should be put before the staff at the emergency meeting, Shannon began to calm down. His whole attitude was a source of strength to her and she was thankful he was here to handle things, to take control.

Impulsively, Shannon decided she wanted Cliff to take over the proceedings entirely. There was no question that he was the person who would be able to keep everything under control. But how would Jason react? His had always been the position of command. Wouldn't he resent Cliff's intrusion?

Shannon glanced thoughtfully at Jason once again. He hardly seemed to be paying attention to what was being said here. So much—everything—depended on it. If only there were time to discuss it, to talk it over with him. But there wasn't. The staff meeting would be held that very day, and Shannon knew that Cliff was the person to take charge of the situation. Technically, she was the one in the position of authority. But she knew she had no public presence, no power to control and guide a full staff, especially in the present circumstances. Hers was the technical, the scientific and the emotional realm. She reveled in the pursuit of medical knowledge; she gloried in the precious, life-giving moments of childbirth. But to run a hospital, manage the staff and the finances . . . more and more she realized she did not want the role. And she was ready to admit that it did not suit her.

She knew, as she listened to Cliff's calm strategy, that she must make her decision for the good of the staff, regardless of what it would mean to Jason.

"Cliff, you've obviously thought this all out. You know what to do. I want to persuade you to take charge of things during this crisis," Shannon said calmly. Inside she was a storm of feelings, all of them different and all of them strong.

Jason looked up, his face growing even more pale. He said nothing but stood up, shakily.

"Excuse me," he said, but before he reached the door he collapsed on the floor in a heap.

"Jason!" Shannon cried, sick with the sudden realization that he was a victim, too.

She ran to his side. "Jason!" But he was out cold, and with a shudder of dread, Shannon noted his gray skin and the telltale splotches.

Chapter 13

Within minutes Jason was put in the isolation ward. In the hall outside his room, Cliff took Shannon by the shoulders. "I know how you feel," he said intensely, looking her in the eyes. "And I wish there were time for feelings. But there isn't. You may never forgive me for what I am going to say—I'm sure you'll see me as an unfeeling beast, but it has to be said. Listen, Shannon, you have to forget about Jason for now. It's time to meet with the others. Don't worry—I'll take charge of the situation for the time being. But I'll need your help, yours more than anyone else's. Do you understand?"

He shook her, gently, and forced her to look into his eyes. "Yes," Shannon whispered. But for the life of her, she didn't know how she was going to be able to carry on.

"And do you know why?" he asked.

Shannon shook her head.

"Because you're an amazing person, that's why. You're a constant marvel," he added with a smile.

Big tears rolled down Shannon's cheeks. Sometimes Cliff reminded her of her grandfather. *Thank God*, she thought. *Thank God he didn't live to see this happen.*

"Now—business." Cliff interrupted her thoughts. "While the staff is gathering for the meeting, I'm going to call Cairo. I want you to collect yourself as much as possible. I'm not saying to stop feeling what you're feeling, because I know you can't. But, I don't want the staff to see any signs of stress. It's not going to be easy, but I know you can do it."

Shannon nodded. She would try. She would try as hard as she could. Cliff smiled understandingly and squeezed her hand. Then he turned and hurried down the hall. She followed him with her eyes until she saw him disappear around a corner. She leaned back against the wall and breathed deeply several times. Now and then an image of Jason, collapsed on the floor, would come to her mind and a sob would catch in her throat. She forced herself to think of other things. She concentrated on her breathing. Slowly, she began to feel in control of herself.

Moments later she was in the comforting familiarity of her office, with its routine and organization and no sign whatsoever of a crisis. Shannon calmly sounded the bell to signal the beginning of the meeting. The ring echoed through the empty corridors like a mournful death knoll.

THE MEETING WENT BETTER than she had expected. Everyone on the staff was informed of the situation, and they responded immediately to Cliff's overall plan and began getting ready for the long fight. They had been silent in the face of Cliff's astounding announcement, and each one had gone to work calmly; if they were feeling panic, they weren't showing it. The word had gone out to all news media, and now the eyes of the world were trained on the little private clinic in Aswan.

Almost immediately, the requested serum and vaccine were collected in Cairo, but there wasn't nearly enough. The Egyptian government obviously couldn't provide the ammunition to combat the deadly disease on its own, and it sent out a desperate call for help to the nations of the world to come to the aid of the Mallison Foundation.

In spite of the various medicines and other treatments the doctors had given Dr. Hinawi's patient, she died painfully and grotesquely in her sleep during the night. Ella, who was being looked after day and night by her nurse, Ann Clark, remained in a semi-comatose state. Jason was rallying well, fluctuating between moments of consciousness and unconsciousness.

For two long days, no new outbreaks of the disease occurred. Shannon had begged Carol to stay at home and not to go to town, under any circumstances, without first going through decontamination procedures. Seeing the growing fear on the faces of Nadah and some of the other servants, Shannon had instructed Yassef to tighten up the night watch so that no one would try to escape.

In spite of all their precautions, two new cases broke out on the fourth day of their exhausting battle, an intern in Jason's ward and one of the servants in the staff quarters. At the clinic everyone waited with bated breath for the next plane from Cairo, which would bring the necessary life-giving serum.

The plague spared no one. In town, the son of the first victim had contracted the disease. The authorities decided to hospitalize the boy at the Mallison Foundation rather than send him to the public hospital and risk infecting the patients there.

Despite all their efforts, the disease began to spread more and more rapidly until there were fourteen cases under Cliff's care. Ann Clark and Stella Drake fell ill and Carol, who spent her entire day watching the comings and goings of the various staff members, seemed upset when she heard the news. Every night, she watched Shannon return home, drained and exhausted from long hours of grueling work. But Carol did little more than watch. It seemed that she was the only one at the Foundation who hadn't thrown herself into the fight.

One night followed the next. Then one night, with an exhausted voice drained of emotion, Shannon whispered to Carol that Jason was dead. But for Shannon it was a night like any other. The work had to go on.

She was caring for an old woman in consultation with Bechir and Divina the next morning. She started violently when Carol walked into the quarantined area. "Carol!" she exclaimed, trying to keep her voice down so as not to disturb her patient. "What on earth are you doing here?"

Ignoring her question, Carol calmly looked around the huge room. It reeked of disinfectant and the fetid odors of diseased bodies. "Give me something to do," she said simply. "If I can't help in some way, I think I'm going to go nuts."

Shannon sensed that her stepsister was fighting some inner battle. She knew it had taken a lot of courage for Carol to come to this particular room. "Go help Farah in the sterilization room," Shannon advised quickly. "There's plenty of work you can do there."

"No, I want to work here, where I can be useful," the younger woman protested.

"Be reasonable, Carol. You haven't been well lately. You . . . ."

"I would only be taking the same risks as everyone else, wouldn't I?" she insisted.

"Yes, but . . . ."

"I've been vaccinated against . . . it, haven't I?"

"Yes, of course, but I don't want to take chances Carol. We don't have enough serum to go around if—if . . . ."

"Oh, what the hell does it matter?" Carol interrupted impatiently. "I want to work here—and no one is going to stop me!"

"All right, then. Put on a smock and come sit by this woman. Keep bathing her forehead and lips with fresh water and see that she doesn't pull out that needle in her arm. It's feeding her the serum she needs. If she gets agitated call Divina and she'll help you."

A little later, Cliff heard about Carol's decision. "You were right not to send her away, Shannon," he commented. "I think she had to do this to ease her conscience. I don't think she could have lived with herself otherwise. However, I'm not sure her health can stand up under the strain."

"Well, whatever happens, I think she's broken through something by deciding to do this—and I don't think we have the right to stop her from helping. She had to do this. It was like some kind of a test . . . and she's passing with flying colors."

Unfortunately, Carol's brave stand came to an end all too soon. That evening, when the nurse came to relieve her, Carol fainted in her arms.

When Shannon heard the news she ran to Carol's bedside and sat up with her all night as she tossed and turned, burning up with a terrible fever and caught in the grips of terrifying nightmares. As the pale light of dawn filtered into the room, Shannon was afraid her stepsister wasn't going to make it. Cliff came to see how Carol was doing. He agreed with Shannon's diagnosis, but he couldn't understand why she wasn't responding to the vaccination and other treatment. She seemed to be getting worse instead of better, and had developed serious secondary complications. "Go and get some rest," Cliff said to Shannon. "I'll stay here with her for a while."

Throwing a despairing glance at her young stepsister, whose lips were dry and parched with fever, Shannon looked up at him and shook her head. "I can't leave her, Cliff. I want to be right here with her, just in case she needs me."

Cliff nodded silently. "All right. Let me know if you want a break," he offered quietly, patting Shannon gently on the shoulder.

Shannon thanked him, but didn't take eyes off Carol. The younger woman was having difficulty breathing. Her face was ashen, swollen almost beyond recognition and badly disfigured by the unmistakable marks of the plague. Shannon took the hands of the dying girl in hers.

"Are we alone?" Carol whispered hoarsely.

"Yes," Shannon replied.

"Before I die, I've got to tell you something, Shannon. I wanted to kill you. I was jealous, because . . . I loved Jason. I wanted him all for myself."

Shannon was thunderstruck by Carol's whispered admission and wondered if she was delirious.

As if she could read Shannon's thoughts, Carol said quietly, "I'm not delirious. I know exactly what I'm saying. I loved Jason from the first moment I met him. But there's something else you should know. He wanted the hospital—that's why he . . . he didn't love you. He . . . he . . . ."

For a moment, Carol seemed unable to go on, and Shannon wasn't sure she wanted to hear any more. But Carol struggled to continue speaking.

"You should know that he wanted *me*, too. He en tried to . . . ." Carol gasped for breath, her hands clenching spasmodically. Her next words came out in a hoarse whisper.

". . . when you were in Cairo. But Bechir . . . . There's worse, worse," she whispered.

Carol's voice began to fade and Shannon leaned over so she could hear her more clearly.

"The scorpion that stung me . . . I bought it from that man at the party. I bought two of them. One I planned to kill you with. I put it on your bed. You were sleeping. But it didn't kill you. Why?"

Shannon remained calm. She didn't react at all to Carol's confession, although inside she was deeply shocked.

"I wanted to tell you," Carol said, a despairing light in her eyes. "I'm sorry. I wanted . . . a new life. Please forgive me," she cried suddenly, mustering the last vestiges of her failing strength. "Forgive me for what I've done to you."

Carol looked up at Shannon, her eyes already clouded with death, and breathed a long, racking sigh. Her head turned slightly on her pillow and she was dead.

Shannon stood there looking down on her step-sister's face. She couldn't cry. She felt only the fuzzy apathy of extreme emotional shock. *Death is the only thing you can depend on*, she thought, miserably, and turned and left the room.

THE DAY AFTER CAROL'S DEATH, Divina, who had been working day and night without a thought for her own health, woke up at dawn feeling totally exhausted and drained of all energy. She was at the end of her strength and courage and felt she just couldn't go on any longer. At first, she thought she was just overworked and paid no attention to her aching head and exhausted body. Convinced she would feel better as the morning progressed, she decided to continue with her work.

She wasn't hungry and, going without breakfast, she hurried to the hospital to begin another grueling day. Before long, however, she realized that she was shivering with fever. She realized she might have contracted the plague and her heart constricted painfully in her chest.

At ten o'clock, she felt too sick to go on and left her patients without saying a word to anyone. She went straight to Cliff's office. He had spent the entire night sitting up with his patients and was now grabbing a quick nap on a cot set up in his office. As Divina came in, he wakened with a start. When he saw her haggard features and her white, bloodless lips, he leaped to his feet.

"Divina, what's the matter?"

She stood in the doorway, leaning against the wall, almost fainting. She looked over at him sorrowfully. "You can't lie when you're facing death," she said, with difficulty.

Cliff moved across the room and gathered her up in his arms. When she regained consciousness much later, she was stretched out on the little cot and the rosy light of twilight was flooding into the office. Cliff had loosened her clothes and covered her with a blanket. He was still there, sitting next to her, looking fondly down into her pale face.

"You frightened me there for a minute," he said calmly. "I thought you had the plague."

She still felt weak but, much to her surprise, realized she was feeling better.

"You're all right, Divina. It's not the plague. You're overworked, that's all," he assured her. "You've overextended yourself since the epidemic started."

"How long have I been out?"

"Well, it's getting dark out now. All afternoon . . . but you needed it. I'd like to give you a sedative, as well."

Divina closed her eyes and sighed. Her lithe, young body gave every appearance of health and well-being, and yet she knew she was dangerously overworked.

"Okay," she said, swallowing the tablets he offered. She looked up at Cliff and smiled. "I guess I haven't been too friendly, have I?" she said. "I owe you an apology."

Cliff wanted to ask a million questions, to say a million things, but when he saw the tears streaming down her face, he found himself moving slowly toward her.

"Please don't cry," he said softly. "I understand."

"Does love always hurt this much?" she asked. "Does the pain ever go away?"

Cliff wiped her tears away and reached for her hand.

Just then he heard the door open behind him. "Pardon me," a woman's voice exclaimed. Cliff knew before he turned that it was Shannon.

"Don't leave. Please."

Shannon said nothing. She turned toward the door, her hand on the knob. In the past few weeks, she and Cliff had been very close. After Carol's outburst, Shannon had needed someone to talk to, someone to help her out of the shock, someone to help her make sense of a life that had turned its ugly face to her like a cruel joke . . . . Someone she could trust and believe in.

Shannon looked around the office. Divina was on the cot, her face flushed, her clothes disheveled, and Cliff was holding her hand. There was little else for her to think but that this man, too had deceived her. She wanted to cry but she held back the tears, afraid that if she spoke or moved she would break down uncontrollably. Vaguely she heard his voice, but she refused to listen; she didn't want to her any more lies. During the endless days and nights of death and pain, she had learned all too well how to shut out the world when she needed to, to regain her sense of dignity and peace. It was the only way to survive.

Cliff's strong, masculine hands grabbed her shoulders. "Look at me, Shannon," Cliff said, his voice calm and deep. "Listen to what I'm saying. Yes, there is a relationship between Divina and me. There has always been a relationship, but it's not what you think. Divina, would you explain, please?"

"Cliff is my guardian, Shannon," Divina said quietly.

"Divina's an orphan, too, Shannon," Cliff said gently. "You have to understand that. Instead of a grandfather she had only me. I love her—I won't say I don't—but like a brother. I've loved her since she was a little girl."

Shannon looked from one face to the other, wanting to trust them yet somehow afraid. How could she believe what they were saying? They had been lying to her from the day she hired them.

"When you came in just now," Cliff continued, "Divina and I were beginning to take down a fence that has been between us for a while now."

Divina nodded in agreement with Cliff's words.

"Well, don't let me bother you. I have to go," Shannon said stiffly, feeling extremely uncomfortable.

"No," Divina said. "Don't go! I want you to hear what I'm going to say. It's important to me that you know . . . that you believe me. I have noticed how important you are to Cliff."

The girl was insistent, and Shannon sat down reluctantly.

"The problem started at the clinic in France. I fell in love with an intern who, I now realize, was a drug addict. He was stealing drugs from the hospital and selling them—or so Cliff tried to tell me, but I wouldn't have any of it. Then he got arrested on a robbery charge. I see now that Cliff was afraid I would be asked to testify, and maybe even charged as an accomplice. He could also see how blinded I was by my . . . my love. That's why Cliff was in such a hurry to get out of France. And that's why I haven't been speaking to him. My heart was broken and I blamed Cliff for it."

Shannon turned and looked at Cliff. He seemed pleased by Divina's words. Shannon guessed that this was the first time Divina had said any of this. Cliff must have suffered, thinking Divina didn't understand why he had done what he had done. Shannon sympathized. She thought of Carol and remembered the horror of seeing someone disintegrating day by day. Only in Divina's case, it was worse, much worse; Divina was innocent.

"But I still don't understand why you didn't just explain the relationship. Why did you lie to me?"

"Well," Cliff responded, "we have to go back a long way for that. Years and years ago, Divina's mother and I were . . . friends, I guess you could say. Edith had had Divina by a previous marriage—she was a widow. Divina was only eight when I first met her, and a little terror, believe me," Cliff added with a beguiling grin. "Divina's great grandfather was a relatively famous scientist—and a Jew. She still carries his name, Berkowitz."

"In France, people who didn't know me thought I was Jewish, because of my name," Divina said. Part of me is, I know, but my father died when I was only a baby and my mother was Protestant. So . . . to me, it was my name and a great grandfather I could brag about to my friends, but that was about it. And I did as much bragging as I could—all kids do. So everyone still thinks I'm Jewish."

"Then your real name isn't Bayeul?"

"I'm afraid it isn't," Cliff interjected. "One

desperate move led to another. When I received your job offer, I knew I had to accept—so I did. The police were getting too close to home. My lawyer suggested that I get Divina out of the country immediately. I was afraid, too, that Divina might try something irrational under all the stress, like running away, or trying to free her boyfriend . . . ."

"And you were right to worry. I was plotting all the time."

Cliff looked at Divina fondly. "It doesn't matter any more," he said. "But to get back to the story," he went on, looking at Shannon. "It was after making the decision and notifying you that it dawned on me there could be problems. That's when Ari offered to get Divina in under another name. Because of his contacts in the government, it was easy for him to arrange. There was no other choice—we had to do it."

"But the future? This deception can't go on forever, can it?" Shannon asked. She was amazed at the story she was hearing, and relieved to finally understand the mystery that had always surrounded Divina and Cliff. Suddenly everything made sense. She could see the angry, heartbroken woman retreating into a shell—an emotional protection that had given her an aura of mystery and aloofness. Seeing the new Divina, a warm, open and beautiful young woman, Shannon couldn't help but like her. She began to understand the terrible burden Cliff had been carrying. It must have been terrible for him to have been hated by someone he loved—someone who was virtually a sister to him. Shannon admired the stand he had taken. He had had to do what he knew was best for Divina, even though he knew she might never forgive him for it.

"Divina," Shannon ventured hesitantly, "why have you changed your attitude? What happened to make you see that Cliff had been right?"

Divina's face clouded. She looked drowsy and upset. "I was afraid you would ask me that. And— and I suppose I must answer."

Divina sighed deeply and turned away from Cliff's gaze. He had an expectant and somehow frightened look.

"Jed—that was my boyfriend's name—contacted me here in Aswan and tried to talk me into stealing some drugs from the hospital. Just this once, he said, just to help him raise the money for his legal battle. At that time I was confiding in Carol a lot—she was approachable and I needed someone to talk to. I didn't tell her everything, but I did tell her about Jed, and being in love and all that.

"So, when Jed was trying to talk me into this drug deal, I told her about it, and I told her I wasn't going to do it. In fact, I was upset that he had even asked. I still thought of him as a good-looking intern I went to the movies with—not as the head of some big dope ring. And I left it at that. When I heard about the problems in the supply room I knew there could be only one person responsible—Carol. But it was a long time before I found out what had really happened.

"Finally I got a letter from Jed. He didn't come right out and say anything, because it would be dangerous for him to have it in writing, but in a private sort of code he had taught me he said that Carol had owed him a lot of money and he wondered if there was some way to get it back, out of her estate or something. I couldn't believe his nerve. That was when I finally figured it all out . . . . What a fool I was! He was using me and I never blinked an eye . . . . Emotions can do funny things."

At that Divina burst into tears again, her body giving way to her pathetic sobs.

There were tears in Shannon's eyes as well. Divina had been through a lot. It would take her a long time to learn to trust and love again, although she was wiser for the experience. *Why can't we ever learn the easy way*, Shannon thought to herself. She wanted to help the other woman, to console her. She wondered what she would do if she had children—how she could help them stay from painful experiences. Was it possible, even?

"There was one thing about that drug theft I couldn't figure out . . . maybe you know," Shannon said finally. "Why were all the order forms written by different people?"

"That was Jed's idea. It was to prevent anyone from tracing the handwriting. So Carol would go into the poor part of town and pay some guy a couple of dollars to sign the things. It was impossible to trace."

Divina yawned and stretched out on the couch.

"You must be feeling the effects of the sedative, Divina," Cliff noted. "You're supposed to be resting—not going through such emotional upheavals. I think we should leave you for a good, long sleep."

Divina laughed lazily. "Hmm. . . sleep would be nice. But about the emotional stuff—I haven't felt this happy in a long time. I'm sad and I hurt, but I'm happy, too. Is that possible? I think things are going to be right again."

Shannon found some pillows and a blanket in the room next door and tucked Divina in. "Rest . . . you've got orders from two doctors now," she said softly, but smiled when she realized that Divina had already slipped into a deep, comfortable sleep.

Outside in the hall, Cliff looked tenderly at Shannon and gathered her into his arms. "My darling, my precious one," he murmured over and over again. "I don't ever want you to be frightened like that again. If you only knew how very much in love with you I am, you would never doubt me."

"Oh, Cliff," Shannon said, bursting into tears. "Why is it that ever since I've known you I've done nothing but cry . . . with joy!"

They looked long and deeply into each other's eyes, basking in the warmth and love that was there for each of them. His finger touching her chin, Cliff tilted Shannon's face toward him and slowly kissed her as if it were the first, last and only kiss on earth. "Marry me, Shannon," he whispered, inhaling her fragrance as if he couldn't get enough of her, holding her closely to him.

And she answered him. "Yes, yes!"

THERE WERE ONLY TWO CASES of the plague in the city during the next few weeks; the epidemic had been contained at the Foundation. Unfortunately, there had been seven deaths. But slowly, the disease ceased to gain ground and, in the first days of November, it died out completely.

A profound feeling of relief swept through the hospital as members of the staff who had fought the disease were finally able to relax. The quarantine was lifted and the doors of the hospital were thrown open once more to the outside world. Slowly, everything returned to normal. They had successfully weathered the storm.

Ari Khalam, sent as a special delegate from his uncle, arrived at the Foundation one day, accompanied by two members of the Health and Welfare committee, to congratulate Shannon, Cliff and the rest of the medical staff for the tremendous work they had done to curb the epidemic. He also announced that, starting immediately, the Foundation would be receiving an annual subsidy from the Egyptian government. Ben Aroual, the proud father of a bouncing baby boy ably delivered by Dr. Hinawi, was one of the first to congratulate Shannon and Cliff. After such a long fight, both of them were tired but happy that their mission had been such a success.

In the days that followed, Shannon and Cliff announced their engagement and decided on a Christmas wedding. Out of respect for the recent deaths of Jason and Carol, the ceremony was to be small and simple. Maturer now, wiser because of the hardships she had endured, Shannon was finally coming into the happiness she deserved.

Years later she and Cliff were to look upon those

early years with a mixture of fondness for the memory of their first love, and horror at the crisis they had had to go through together. They shared a life that was full of more happiness and contentment than either had ever dreamed possible. They traveled around the world together, delivering papers at medical conventions, each enjoying the growing celebrity of the other. The Mallison Hospital became more and more respected in the areas of research and surgical expertise. People came from around the world to get treatment that was not available elsewhere.

Divina decided to study abroad, where she met a man, a professor, and she was happily married and living in France. Cliff and Shannon visited her often. For everyone, the past slowly became a vague, irrelevant memory.

But it was the birth of a daughter, Celeste, that became the highlight of Shannon's and Cliff's life. They had been happy before; now they basked in a shared sense of pride and purpose—and the joy of love that was their daily portion.